GIL'S GRIMOIRE, A SHORT PRELUDE:

TWO ZEROS AND
THE LIBRARY OF DOOM!

BY ERIC BONKOWSKI

COPYRIGHT

DEDICATION & GRATITUDE

For my beautiful wife Kathleen, without whom this
would not exist. With my love.

And for my family, whose constant love and
encouragement have gotten me this far and will help
carry me further.

***

Special thanks to my friend Dean Kotz and the gift
of his magnificent art.

And to all the proofreaders.

ALSO BY THE AUTHOR:

Two Zeros and The Library of Doom!

The Zeros and The Man Who Could Not Die

The Zeros and The Empirical Evidence of Stars
(forthcoming)

Brick Brannigan is Knee-Deep in Peril!

Brick Brannigan is Buried Alive in the Faroe Islands!
(forthcoming)

A NOTE TO THE READER:

At this end of this novella is a sample chapter from *The Zeros and The Man Who Could Not Die*, the first full-length novel of the Zeros, available now from Penny Dreadful Publications. Visit http://www.gilsgrimoire.com for more information.

Now, that's enough delay. On with our tale...

GIL'S GRIMOIRE, A SHORT PRELUDE:

TWO ZEROS AND THE LIBRARY OF DOOM!

"History is a bath of blood."
- William James

CHAPTER 1. THIS PLACE IS EMPTY

Gil was the first through the hulking behemoth of a front door; it swung open with a groan that sounded like an elephant sighing. Huge brass lion heads were mounted at the center of each door, iron rings dangling from their mouths. "Big knockers," Gil chuckled.

Wait a second and let me explain, begging your pardon on behalf of my boss–a man who's actually come to be a good friend. The first thing you need to understand is that Gil Abercrombie can't help himself. Exuberantly youthful billionaire, monster hunter, action figure collector, comic book reader, Lego builder–and yeah, I did say monster hunter. Quite a combo to bring together in the package of a fifty-something old guy with a bushy mustache. He's a grown man, or so his AARP card claims.

My name is Dylan, former police officer, soldier, and private security specialist. Over the years I've learned that I'm good with my hands, guns, and knives. Recently I've been forced to add swords, maces, pikes, axes, and even the quarterstaff to my already respectable skill set. It was just such a skill set that got me hired not long ago by Gil as his new heavy. Essentially, I drive the car, cook the meals, offer the more grounded reader's perspective, and try to keep my new friends safe. Along with Gil's partner, Alistair Finch, we make up what we affectionately refer to as the Zeros: three guys worth nothing to no one (except each other and our portfolio manager–in Gil's case, at least). A bit dramatic, perhaps, but true enough. Anyway, we get in scrapes with monsters and nasties of all kinds. Gil would say we're heroes. At first, I thought it was a little weird. I'm okay with it now. Gil's the heart, Finch is the brain, and I'm the guy who breaks stuff. Anyway, back to the big scary house and our tale that is already in progress.

Built from faded red bricks and covered with ivy that looked more like veins on a weightlifter's forearm, the mansion and one time sanatorium was called Callowleigh, and its history since being shut down by the state was more sordid than its current state of disrepair.

"Any thought you had to using magic in this dump, you better shelve it right now, big man. I'm getting all kinds of weird feelings in here," Gil said, pulling wide tangles of spiderwebs out of the air.

Ahh, yes, magic. Let's just say that magic and I were reluctant bedfellows, currently embroiled in a bit of a love/hate relationship. All I'll say right now is that it's complicated. I don't want to talk about it. "No magic, huh? I can live with that," I said, stepping into the foyer behind Gil and giving the huge door a push, letting it shut behind me with a

2

puff of stale air. "I'd be afraid the place would come down around us if we tried."

"Probably would," Gil said. "If the roof comes down, do me a solid and catch it before it hits me in the head, would ya?" From inside his coat–a plaid professor's jacket with elbow patches and a button on his lapel that read "BAZINGA!"–Gil pulled a pipe and slipped it into his mouth. He tamped down the tobacco, his coat opening to reveal an Iron Maiden t-shirt beneath. A match snapped lit, opening a small halo of light in the dark foyer before it disappeared into the bell of the pipe. Foul clouds of smoke rose into the air moments later.

The room was massive, leading off to at least a half-dozen halls around us. From what I could see, the place still looked fully furnished; a few old-fashioned chaise lounges decorated the open entryway, plush oriental carpeting beneath our feet, thick with dust and dirt accumulated over years of neglect. The most impressive part of the room, however, lay dead ahead of us.

"Holy moly," Gil said.

A grand staircase, crimson-carpeted and at least fifteen feet wide, rose up before us, leading toward what looked to be a mezzanine. My eyes followed it upward to a broad stained-glass window that overlooked the entire room. A crash of lightning outside illuminated the brightly colored mosaic: an image of Christ on the cross at Golgotha.

"That's… dramatic," I muttered. Thunder rumbled in agreement.

"Dramatic? It's freakin' scary to see that thing when you first walk in. A gigantic crucifixion scene? Welcome to Callowleigh, enjoy some tea and ritual execution while you recover from surgery."

Callowleigh, previously known as the Callowleigh Retreat for Surgical Recovery and Recuperation, was our new job. More specifically, finding the missing caretaker was our new job. The Zeros had been hired by a business partner and on-again-off-again client Eleanor Robbes-Grillet, Callowleigh being just one of about a million properties in and around Philadelphia she owned. In this case, the grand old mansion retreat was a few miles out the Pennsylvania Turnpike, nestled in the quiet Amish country of Lancaster County.

"Let's find this guy and get out of here," I said, my voice a whisper. I swallowed, I was a little more frightened than I should have been. Whatever, I'd seen enough already to know that big dark houses look scary for a reason. Thunder rumbled again.

"You wanna get out of here? I'm ready to kill to get out of here. There's a *Hercules: The Legendary Journey* marathon that starts at ten. Let me tell you, big man, I plan on being there when it happens. We're probably gonna find this old-timer reading back issues of Reader's Digest in the bathroom."

Gil took the first step of the grand staircase, the wood beneath the matted carpeting creaking. I gave him a minute, looking around the room and trying

4

not to make eye contact with giant Roman soldier or giant Saint Peter.

The sound of rumbling thunder almost masked another sound that shuddered behind me. It sounded like the shaking and creaking of metal parts, like loose gears or hinges. I turned to look over my shoulder, freezing as I saw a blur of motion in one of the darkened hallways.

"Hold on," I said. From beneath my own coat, I pulled a heavy Maglite flashlight and clicked it on, passing the beam of clear white light over the wall on the eastern face of the room.

"What is it, you see something? Hey you got a flashlight? That's not fair." Gil muttered, his voice uneasy.

"You know, for a billionaire, you are sorely lacking in supplies."

"What do you mean? I brought my Gameboy."

The wall was covered with a sick green wallpaper that had nebulous shapes on it like rotten paisleys. Over certain stretches of wall, the green paper was torn and hanging in tattered strips. A few dark splotches stained the plaster beneath the ripped paper. Large, framed pictures or paintings hung at uneven intervals, each covered with a dusty drop cloth. Something about the jagged rips looked more than random to my eyes.

"Are those…?"

"No," Gil said firmly. "No, no, no. I don't want to say that. Not yet. Absolutely not. Those are not...

claw marks. They can't be. *Hercules*, remember? Ten o'clock? When I agreed to do this job for Eleanor, it was because it was easy. This caretaker guy's phone is broken and he doesn't know it. That's why he's been out of touch. We're here to fix his phone and go home. Easy as pie."

"You did give Finch the night off," I said.

"He's got a date for the first time in like two hundred years, so yeah I gave him the night off. This isn't supposed to be super bad, remember?" he said. I couldn't tell if he was convincing me or himself. "This is going to be easy. Our first easy job after almost getting killed by that nutball djinn and the–"

The sound of rattling chain again, silencing Gil. He took a step down towards me. "Did you hear it that time?" I asked.

He moaned. "Uh huh."

I moved the beam of the flashlight further down the wall, the broad circle of light eventually coming to rest on a darkened doorway that I'd originally taken to be a hallway. It was no hall. Instead of a door, the accordion gate of an old elevator barred the entryway. A long chain wound around the gate and looped through holes drilled in the door jamb, holding the gate shut. Beyond the gate there was nothing. The elevator car was missing, revealing only the black shaft.

As we watched, the chain shuddered again, the gate rattling against the chains that bound it shut, as if unseen hands worked to pull it open.

"Whoa, buddy!" Gil said, pulling his pipe from his mouth and taking a step closer to me at the same time that I took a step back. We collided, and I almost knocked him over. He closed a hand on my arm and peered over it, eyes wide.

"What's going on, Boss?" I asked.

"I have no idea," he said.

"Do you want to get out of here? Get some reinforcements? Come back?"

From Gil, I heard a long silence. All around us, the room seemed to be slowly coming to life, sounds beginning to arise from every dark corner. The rattling of chains was only the beginning of it.

At this point–regardless of the fact that I'd only worked with Gil for a couple of weeks–I understood the calculations that were spiraling through his mind as we stood in the center of the mansion foyer. There was a man somewhere in this mansion, an old man, all alone. The old caretaker's name was Edward Dawkins, and he worked as a novice in restoration of historic landmarks. I'd read a little about Callowleigh before we'd come, hoping that the evil that once had such a grip on this grand old place had left it. Either way, the man had a lot of hard work ahead of him. Dawkins had volunteered for the position five weeks earlier, and he made his small salary watching over the terrible structure with its wicked past because no one else–more experience or otherwise–would. With his care and guidance, hopefully something good could come of this place for a change. Without a person who cared, whatever evil that called Callowleigh home would only fester. Gil sighed. Without us, the odds were that this Mr. Dawkins would never step out of Callowleigh alive.

"Boss?" I asked.

"No turning back," he said. He wouldn't, not when an innocent man's life was at stake. I knew he'd say it, and I was okay with it.

"Press on?"

"Press on, big man. It's been a while since I've been in a spooky place like this dump, but oh well, we'll find our way. Just stay close, ya hear?"

"You got it." I turned my light away from the elevator shaft, ignoring the rattling of chains and the whispers that seemed to come up the shaft from below.

It wasn't so hard to ignore those sounds. It was harder to ignore the sounds of countless footsteps on the floors above. Or the squeak of a rusted wheelchair axle turning. Or the distant sounds of laughter.

Together, Gil and I climbed the stairs.

CHAPTER 2. COMPLICATED

At the top of the stairs, we stopped. The mezzanine level must have been where in-patient entry was processed. Large desks were set up at even intervals like check-out lines in a grocery store. Pens and paperwork still cluttered dusty calendars and blotters. It looked like the original staff had simply picked up and walked out one day.

"More creepy," Gil said. "Awesome. Love that." He turned to me and eyed my flashlight enviously. "We better stay close together, big man. You know, for safety's sake."

"I will, don't worry. You think I want to be alone in here?"

He shrugged and started walking, going down one of the entry aisles as if we ourselves were being processed. He stopped at the desk and reached out, taking a partially filled-out sheet of paper from the blotter. A fine layer of dust covered it like peach fuzz. Gil removed the pipe from his mouth, took a deep breath, and blew the dust off. A cloud of dust bunnies circled in the air.

"Would you look at that," he said, pointing.

"This form was filled out in 1957. Good gravy."

"And they just stopped filling the thing out half-way through?"

"It would appear that way."

Not what I would call characteristic of healthcare bureaucrats, either today or in 1957. If you've ever been in a hospital, I think you'd agree. Not a bunch to take paperwork lightly.

"Dylan, how much do you know about this place?" Gil asked.

"I read some stuff before coming. Probably all the same stuff you read, though."

Gil lowered the paper, licking his lips. He smiled before returning the pipe stem to his mouth. Shifting his feet nervously, he said, "Uh, research. Yeah, about that…"

"Hold on, are you serious? You haven't read *anything* about this place? Not a thing? Didn't prepare or do any research at all? This is a job, Boss."

"It was supposed to be really super easy, so–"

"So you just mailed it in?"

"No, no. What? I didn't *mail* anything in. People don't use the mail anymore, man, that expression is dead. Anyway, Finch…"

"Finch what?"

"Well, Finch usually does this bit."

"What do you mean?"

"Like the intel, the prep, the smart stuff. You

know. I mean, I know about monsters and how to fight monsters and what monsters can't eat chocolate or don't respond well to bug spray. And swords, I know about swords. And *Star Wars*. But Finch? I mean, yeah, he does the smart stuff."

"Oh man." When I'm the brains in an operation, that's not good. Remember, I usually just break stuff.

"I'm sorry, Dylan. I mean, I guess I should've known better the second we got here and saw the **CONDEMNED** sign. Not to mention the **KEEP OUT** one, the **POLICE LINE, DO NOT CROSS** one. And that other one."

"What other one?"

"You know, that big freaky serial-killer-lookin' spray-painted one nailed to the tree."

Oh boy. "I didn't see that one, Boss."

"Well, it said **KEEP OUT, THE DEVIL LIVES HERE**."

"What? That didn't give you some hint of otherworld foul play?"

"It coulda just been some crazy kids. It coulda been a lot of things, really. But, I mean, crazy kids playin' tricks? Don't you ever watch *Scooby Doo*?"

"Boss, I haven't seen that show since I was about nine years old."

"I watched a few episodes a couple of days ago, and this kind of thing happens all the time on *Scooby Doo*. And it's always fine on there. It's usually just some crazy kids being, you know, crazy. Or," he raised a finger and wagged it at me. "Or it's the caretaker. You know how often it's the lonely old man caretaker on there? Maybe it's the caretaker this time, too."

"I thought we were here to *rescue* the caretaker."

"Oh. Yeah. Well, it's probably not the caretaker then. But, the kids. There's always the kids."

I sighed. "I know, the crazy kids. Let's go, please," I urged. Thunder rumbled and a flash of lightning lit the room for a second. We were standing just beneath a huge crucifixion stained-glass window, talking about devil stuff, and listening to mysterious chains rattling and the sounds of phantom laughter. If there was a time and place to talk about *Scooby Doo*, this was not it.

"So are you gonna tell me about this place?" he asked.

"Maybe. Let's just keep moving, all right? At this point, I don't know if it would matter anyway. Clearly this place is haunted."

"Haunted's not really the word for this, I don't think. I think it's a little more complicated."

I gave him a good push, urging him along. "Well you can correct my choice of words if we keep moving. Right now, I'm ready to pick you up and carry you if I have to."

***

I'd never been the Finch in the group before, but it was exhausting. Basically I'd become the Mom of the bunch, and it wasn't much fun. Gil was more easily distracted than a six-year-old cranked up on Mountain Dew.

The in-patient processing room led the way to six parallel waiting rooms connected to six examination rooms. Each was fully furnished and stocked with sixty-year-old medical supplies that Gil proceeded to play with. The only other recent visitor seemed to be the dust fairy.

"What kind of place is this?" Gil asked, squeezing a cracked rubber blood pressure pump idly. "And it's so friggin' big. The volume of patients that they must have had, or at least expected."

"Well, it opened in '45," I said.

"So the war." He nodded, dropping the old pump. "Makes sense. There would have been a lot of people in need of physical rehab. Psychological, too."

"Business here must've slowed down a lot in the years following."

He ran a finger along a dusty tabletop and frowned at it. "I'd say."

We walked through an exam room, coming out the other side into what looked like a big lounge. Small circular tables were spread around the room, as well as long couches and a few matching chairs. On the north wall the room, wide windows overlooked an overgrown courtyard. Lightning flashed again, illuminating a muddy, lily pad-filled pond in the center. I turned away from the window, surveying the room. It was the first that showed signs of a real disturbance.

A few of the chairs were overturned and at least one table was broken. What was disconcerting was the fact that it was wrought iron. It lay in a twisted knot on the floor like a discarded clump of black licorice.

Then there was the blood.

In a wide, explosive splatter on the east wall of the room, a Rorschach test of gore was sprayed across a wide stretch of plain white wall between a pair of doorways. There was definitely an impact mark in the center–a place where the plaster drywall had cracked and been crushed inward–and a wide swatch of blood pooled on the floor beneath. Everything was dry, as I imagine it'd happened very long ago. You know, circa 1957.

"How did this place close again?" Gil asked in a whisper.

"I didn't read that far," I admitted. "But I don't think it was amicably."

From the dried pool of blood led a trail, like something had been dragged away. The trail curved into the right hand doorway, disappearing into darkness. My flashlight beam followed it for a few feet until the beam dispersed in shadow. Beyond that, the trail was lost.

"Hey, you got like, a whole bunch of weapons, big man?" Gil asked.

"Hold on, you didn't bring any weapons either? You didn't do any research, and you didn't even bring any weapons, but you brought your gameboy? Why would you–"

The urgent rattling of chains interrupted me. Instinctively, I turned to look behind me, swinging the narrow beam of light over my shoulder.

"Whoa holy smokes, did you hear that?" Gil asked, stepping behind me.

"Was it behind us?"

"No, no it was over there," he pointed to the doorway to the left of the blood splatter.

"Are you sure?"

"Unfortunately," he said. "I think I'd prefer if it came from downstairs. Or, you know, Alaska."

The left-hand door was blocked by a drop cloth like the paintings that hung on the walls downstairs. I leveled my flashlight on it. The two of us held our breath as the sounds of chains stopped as quickly as they'd started. The circle of light hung on the pale cotton sheet, shaking gently in my unsteady hand.

Nothing happened. The only things I could hear were Gil's heavy breathing–he sounded like a fat guy who had just run the 50 yard dash–and the thunder rumbling outside.

Gil nudged me. "Go check it. Look behind that curtain."

"Hey screw you man, you go check it."

The cloth fluttered. Only slightly at first, as if there was a faint draft, then more so. It lifted off the door frame like a gentle breeze was blowing, revealing the same accordion elevator gate as we'd seen in Callowleigh's entryway.

"Shit, another elevator shaft. How many elevators are in this place?" I asked.

"I dunno. At least it's handicap accessible," Gil said.

The sheet lifted again, higher this time, revealing the same wrapped chains we'd seen downstairs, holding the gate closed.

"Why are the elevator shafts all locked and sealed?" I asked.

"Better question: where are all of the elevator cars?"

Another gust of air blew the drop cloth back, the sheet rising until it was almost parallel to the floor. Gil was right. Behind the gate, the shaft was empty. No car. No nothing. The draft carrying the sheet was strong enough to reach us this time. The air was hot and sickly wet, like a blast of rank morning breath.

"Is this typical for a haunted house?" I asked.

"Remember when I said I think this is more complicated than that? Yeah, I think it's more complicated than that." He pointed. "Look."

I lowered the flashlight, illuminating footprints in dust on the hardwood floor. They led into the right-hand doorway, following the bloody trail.

"You think it's Dawkins?"

Gil gulped. "I don't really wanna think about the alternative. Also, I was pointing at *that*." He gestured with an unsteady hand.

I moved the light. About ten inches or so to the right of the footprints was another marking. It was a narrow line, like something being dragged, like a rope or, well, or a *chain*. It mirrored the footprints perfectly. If those tracks were Dawkins' then he had been followed. By something that didn't walk on two feet.

"Maybe it's like a Jacob Marley ghost, or something." I said, my voice shaking. "You know, he drags chains and doesn't walk because he's a ghost? Is that a real thing?"

"I dunno. I'm still going with the caretaker. Yeah, it's just the caretaker."

"Don't you mean crazy kids?"

He gulped. "Yeah, of course. The crazy kids."

"I hope you're right."

Slowly, we started down the hallway, following the dusty footprints and the bloody trail. A few feet down the hall, my light landed on the form of an overturned wheelchair. One wheel spun lazily. More blood was pooled on the floor. This blood looked wet. Fresh.

"Oh, damn," I muttered.

Somewhere ahead, a door slammed.

CHAPTER 3. CAN'T YOU HEAR ME KNOCKING?

At the end of the hallway were a pair of double doors, propped open. Through the doors was a huge open space, its walls shrouded in shadow. Our footsteps echoed across the wood floor. At the other end of the room was a locked door, presumably the same door that had slammed. The blood trail that we were following continued under it and beyond.

"Guess Eleanor didn't give you any keys, did she?" I asked.

"Actually, she did."

"Ah, so let it not be said that you came totally empty-handed."

"Ha, ha, hey you're pretty funny for a big bald guy," Gil said as he pulled a ring from a deep coat pocket and gave it a dramatic shake. Some of the keys were halfway modern looking. Most weren't.

"For the record, I shave my head."

"Oh yeah, sure," he said as he stooped, casting an uneasy glance over his shoulder, and began fitting keys unsuccessfully into the lock. The door was tall and–unlike the others we'd seen–was made of dull unfinished metal. While Gil fiddled with the lock, I turned, keeping a wary eye on the spooky wheelchair at the far end of the room–and our backs.

The room we were in was long and wide, and the main expanse of the space was clear of furniture. The floor was a well-finished, glossy hardwood floor, constructed from long parallel rows of narrow wooden slats. High above us were long, peaked skylights showing the black night sky beyond. A slow rain had begun falling, pattering on the glass. Between the floor and the skylight, I didn't have a hard time imagining what the room probably was: a gymnasium. In the corner was a doorway leading downward. I aimed the flashlight beam at the doorway, illuminating a sign.

"Hey, I was right," I said.

"What?"

"Oh, sorry, just thinking out loud. That sign in the corner says 'Pool–Lower Level.' We must be in the gym or something."

"So the bleachers didn't clear that up for you?"

I turned the beam against the walls, illuminating long rows of old wooden bleachers. Beneath them ran dark expanses of shadow that the beam of the flashlight did little to penetrate.

"Oh."

"Yeah I'm not too wild about a giant open space that is this dark," Gil said. "I have an old habit of checking walls and corners first. Shadows are not my friend."

"Tell me about it."

At the far end of the room we heard the sound of a door slamming again. The sound echoed through the huge open space. Slow footsteps began tapping across the floor, coming towards us.

"Zoinks, big man," Gil said, straightening up and coming to my side, our backs to the locked door.

"Boss, I am not liking this." I turned the beam into the empty space at the center of the gym, light passing over nothing but dusty hardwood.

The footsteps stopped.

"Maybe the invisible man stopped for a quick dip?" Gil murmured, waving his hand towards the steps leading down to the pool.

We waited, but the steps were gone.

"Want me to check for footprints?" I asked.

"I want you and Mr. Flashlight to stay right here with me," Gil said, turning and trying again to get the door open, this time with urgency.

"Okay, well, hold this," I said, handing him the flashlight. He took it, his hand shaking.

I walked out into the middle of the floor, right around where the center circle would be on a basketball court. When I got there, I stopped and listened.

I heard the rain. I heard the thunder rumbling overhead and the wind in the trees. I heard the Boss's key ring jingling behind me as he nervously struggled with the lock. Really, the inside of the gym was quiet. I don't want to say *too quiet*, but it was pretty damn quiet.

The sound started very faintly, as if it was coming from a great distance. It grew, but very slowly.

"Quiet, Boss," I said after a minute. The jingling of keys ceased.

"What is it?"

"Listen."

It was subtle. For a minute, I thought it was my imagination. I closed my eyes, focusing. After a moment, I heard it again, steadily growing.

"I hear somethin'," Gil said.

"*Shhh*," I said.

At first, it sounded like two pieces of paper being slid against each other. Then it changed, the timbre becoming something more akin to soft tapping. Steady tapping. I took a few steps toward the sound, trying to piece together what it was exactly.

"Dylan, get back."

"Hold on, Boss. I think..."

"Get back, I said."

"Wait." I took another few steps into the darkness. Behind me, Gil was trying to follow me with the beam of the flashlight, but we were too far apart.

"Dylan," he urged. "Come back, please."

The sound continued, slow and steady. Somehow, my curiosity was trumping my better judgement, to say nothing of fear.

"It's just up here," I said softly.

"Don't."

I stopped, almost fully enshrouded in darkness. It wasn't tapping, it was shaking. Rattling. The sound came out to meet me, a hollow sound, almost like a cheap plastic maraca.

But it wasn't a maraca.

"Dylan, get back here!" Gil shouted.

"Hold on, that can't be a..."

"It's a goddamn rattlesnake, man!!"

Gil was swinging the light around like mad as he abandoned the door and ran towards me, light playing off the ceiling and floor and bleachers. I was frozen, listening to the snake's rattling tail approach and realizing how stupid I had been. *This is what happens when you get a little too brave working with these guys*; the detached thought floating through my head.

"Dylan!"

I took a step back as Gil's light finally landed on the shiny russet and olive scales of the snake, coiled a few feet from me. Slowly, it's head rose, a long forked tongue flicking from between its open jaws.

"Take a step back, big man, nice and slow," Gil was saying. He stood a few paces behind me, hands raised like he was being robbed at gunpoint.

"I am. Just quiet down. Calm, Boss. Be calm..." I said.

I took a few steps back, my eyes locked on the snake's. I'm sure it was my imagination, but they seemed to be glowing.

I bumped into Gil and together the two of us began stumbling backwards. Until we heard it again. Now the rattling was in stereo.

"I coulda sworn that wasn't there a second ago," Gil said, his voice wavering.

"You gotta be kidding me."

"It's behind me, like four feet maybe? I'd like to say it's got a lollypop, but actually... it looks kinda pissed. Can we go another direction, please?"

I turned, seeing the coiled shape of a second snake, identical to the first. Jaws wide, tongue flicking, fangs menacing. Unlike the first snake, however, it was uncoiling as it slid toward us.

"To the left," I said, tugging Gil's arm. "Left, left!"

We hustled to the left, awkwardly stumbling like a three-legged racer, Gil swinging the flashlight towards the pair of snakes that were now both slithering towards us.

"Up on the bleachers," I said. "Climb up!"

"No, wait!" We skidded to a halt, two more rattlesnakes slipping from beneath the edge of the bleachers.

"Seriously? We're in Pennsylvania, not the friggin' Mojave Desert!"

"Back, go back towards the door," Gil said, handing me the flashlight. We broke into an undignified run, Gil pulling the ring of keys from his pocket again, eyes moving over the blocky silver and bronze keys.

Gil tumbled to his knees in front of the lock, jamming a key into the lock and giving it a turn. No luck. He tried another. Nothing. He swore, glancing over his shoulder.

I swept the circle of light over the floor slowly, waiting. I could hear the approach of the rattlers, coming left, right, and center.

"Open the door, we got some unfriendly company."

"It's this one, it's got to be this one," he said. It wasn't.

"Dammit, Boss..."

"Hold 'em off, big man."

"Easy for you to say!" I said through gritted teeth.

The first snake got within reach of the flashlight, its mouth hanging open, fangs long and curved. The length of its body writhing and twisting, pushing it forward with surprising speed.

The metal flashlight in my hand was all I had. I lunged, swinging the head of the light and catching the snake across the neck, tossing it off into the darkness. It was replaced with two more. I kept swinging.

"Come on!" I begged.

I heard the keys fall from Gil's hand and clatter to the hardwood floor. "Seriously, man?" Gil shouted. He stooped for the keys and snatched them before rising again. Desperate, he pounded on the metal door with one fist before jamming one last key into the hole. "Open sesame, por favor!"

It wasn't the right key, but something *did* happen: something knocked back.

Huge and deep, it echoed through the gymnasium, the impact loud enough and deep enough to shake dust from the high rafters. Gil and I froze, wide-eyed.

The sound hadn't come from the other side of the door. It had come from beneath us. Great and powerful, it was as if a giant fist had cracked against the underside of the floor.

As one, the snakes withdrew, the rattles on their tales suddenly silent.

"What the hell was that?" I asked.

"It came from..."

"...the pool?"

It came again, a terrible crushing boom from beneath us, strong enough to knock us from our feet and sounding like a howitzer launched from the next room. A few boards cracked from the pressure, snapping and stirring up countless plumes of dust. After a moment, another crash. More boards broke. Now it seemed like the entire floor was beginning to bow upward at the center of the room.

"The door, get the DOOR!"

Gil turned, spinning the endless ring of keys and choosing a new one, slipping it into the lock and turning. Still wrong.

"How many keys do you have there?"

"This one, come on baby, be my key!"

The lock, stubborn and rusted, tumbled lethargically in the mechanism. Gil cackled, victorious. He pocketed the ring and pulled. The door didn't budge.

From beneath, the terrible impact sounded again. Boards broke free, coming up and out of the floor and scattering in disarray. From beneath us, I heard a deep, primal roar, so deep and raw as to sound almost geological, like the rumble of a volcano erupting.

"Gil," I said. "The door... please... the *door*..."

The floor rose from center court, large portions of lacquered wood breaking free and tumbling from the *hill* that was slowly rising.

Gil glanced over his shoulder. "Holy cow man, that thing wasn't there a second ago!"

"Gil, open the fucking door!"

I turned, putting my hand over his and pulling. It didn't open, but the door shook with a metal-on-metal *screeech*, opening about a quarter of an inch.

"Again!" I said, bracing myself against the doorframe for leverage. Behind us, I could hear the roar, rising in volume, and the continual cracking as the wood floor exploded in pieces.

Together, we pulled. The door budged again,

but still wouldn't open.

I glanced over my shoulder. From the disintegrating center of the floor, something was emerging, as cracked planks and bent nails flew around us.

"Pull again, Dylan, once more should do it!"

"Holy shit," I muttered.

Gil turned, following my eyes. It wasn't too hard to figure out what I was looking at.

"Holy shit," he echoed.

From the center of the room, a thick vermillion *tentacle* was rising from the gaping hole in the floor. A gaping hole completely punched out, the floor beneath us was beginning to collapse, weakening and beginning to droop, funneling us towards the tentacle.

"Open sesame!" Gil shouted. "It worked once! One more time, pretty please!"

My shoes slipped on the hardwood and I fell to my knees. It took me a second to get back on my feet, one hand on the doorknob, one on Gil. Together, we pulled. The metal groaned again, the door loosening from the jamb's terrible grip.

The roaring behind us rose again, the floor quivering as some fresh hell pushed against it. I heard the cracking of two-by-fours and the moan of I-beams bending. Huge segments of the floor fell, disappearing into the darkness below as a second tentacle rose from the pool and began moving towards us.

"Come on, Boss," I said. "*One more time*."

I grabbed Gil's arm and pulled him up towards the door, his shoes having a harder time finding traction on the floor than my own. The floor beneath us rose, leveling for a moment and giving me the chance to put my shoulder against the door frame and pull.

The door popped open with a *crack*, the frame coming lose from the decayed drywall.

"All right, go, GO!" I pushed Gil through the doorway into another dark corridor, apparently Callowleigh's specialty. Beneath me, the floor gave way, dropping downward towards the pool and landing with a splash. I caught the door handle, the entire frame creaking and groaning, threatening to pull completely free of the wall. My feet pinwheeling, I thought for a moment that I was about to splash down in the monster's baby pool before Gil closed a hand around mine and pulled.

Together, we got my heavy ass up and into the hallway as the last of the gym flooring fell away behind me. I lay on the floor for a second, gasping for air as Gil pulled at my hand.

"Let's go, let's *gooooo*," he crooned. I followed his gaze towards my feet to see a tentacle, as thick as my thigh, pass through the remains of the doorway and move towards me.

"Whoa, whoa, whoa." I kicked my legs and pushed backwards. After a moment, I was on my feet, Gil and I running down the corridor with a tentacle at our heels.

We made the first left and immediately crashed into a pair of wide double doors. The doors swung open, and we collapsed on the floor in a pile.

It was a library, unnaturally well-lit by the warm glow of old tungsten lightbulbs. Books were everywhere; shelved on the cases covering every inch of every wall, piled on tables like leaning towers, heaped in mountains on the floor.

"Well, I didn't see that comin'," Gil said.

CHAPTER 4. SHE SMILED SWEETLY

Neither of us could have guessed that a huge, well-lit, academic library lay at the end of a hallway about ten yards from the gymnasium, but there you have it. As you can imagine, we were a little surprised.

Gil was first on his feet. "Get up," he said. "Help me seal this door."

"EEeeerrgggggghhlllllhh," I said, although I was going for, "One moment please."

"What? Are you tired? Come on, man, there's a killer octomom out there. In a second one of its funky suction cup hands is gonna be creepin' in here to take us back to its pool!"

With effort, I got on my feet, grumbling all the while. Gil got behind one door and pushed. I did the same with the other. They closed, sort of. Something had knocked them out of alignment–probably the combined weight of Gil and I crashing into them at full speed–and they wouldn't latch. Gil and I each put in some elbow grease. Nothing worked.

"Leave it," I said eventually. "If that squid

thing was going to try and reach us here it would have done so already. I figure we're safe enough for now."

Gil shrugged, dejected. "Really, I'd like it better if we could lock this door."

I gave him a good dirty look before grabbing a chair from a nearby table and jamming it beneath the doorknobs. I settled it against the rug and gave the doors a good pull to demonstrate. "There you go," I said. "Locked."

Gil shrugged. "Not really, I mean–"

"Listen Mr. I-don't-do-research and I-don't-even-bring-weapons-because-it's-bound-to-be-so-easy, I think you can throw stones when you *bring* them. Eh?"

"That metaphor's a little thin, don't you think?"

"You brought us to this death trap under the assumption that it was a walk in the park! It has not been a walk in the park! So at least back off on my metaphors, man." Maybe I was a little pissy, but I was mad. Hell, we'd just been attacked by a Kraken in a haunted mansion.

"Hey man, I told you, I'm not the *brains* of the operation, remember? I'm just the–"

A pile of books overturned, tumbling from a table into a cluttered mound on the floor, cutting Gil off mid-sentence.

"Oh shit," he muttered. "We're in a ghost house, remember? Let's argue later."

"Okay," I sighed, turning to face the library.

Surveying the place only made it that much weirder. From where we stood at the entrance, I couldn't see the back wall, the room was that deep. It was at least seventy-five feet wide or so, and its cathedral ceilings and chandeliers made it seem even bigger. Above us was an open second floor, the ornate balustrade winding its way around even more book cases. There were books everywhere.

The main floor had long tables typical of most libraries, although as previously stated, the library's current state would make most librarians want to throw their bodies off the mezzanine.

"It's a freakin' mess in here," Gil said, pointing as if I could not see.

"Yeah, it really is."

He walked over to the closest bookcase and ran his hand along the spines of old tomes, turning his head sideways to read the titles. At the first hole, he looked at the floor, his eyes searching the titles piled at his feet.

"Look at this," he said, picking up a book. *"Treating Shell Shock in the Modern Soldier*, by Charles D. Alderton." He looked at the bookshelf again. "Goes right here," he said, sliding the book back into place.

"So?"

He pulled the book free again. "Look."

I walked over to him and took the book. He was pointing at the line between the faded and unfaded portions of the cover. Like any book that spent years and years on a shelf exposed to sunlight, this old book suffered severe sun damage and fading. I looked up over my shoulder at the grand windows on the second floor above us.

"It's faded," I said.

"Yeah, but look where the line stops," he pointed again.

I shrugged. "So what? It sat there on the ground until the sun faded it."

He slipped the book back onto the shelf. The fading perfectly aligned with the books on either side of it. "See? It got sun faded here on the shelf, not on the floor."

"So it hasn't been on the floor for long."

"Exactly. Someone's been going through the books here. For one reason or another, this book got pulled off the shelf and thrown on the floor."

"Somebody was looking for something? This doesn't look like the work of a caretaker."

Gil laughed. "No kidding. More the work of a care*less* taker. Get it?"

"Uh huh. Clever."

Rather than laugh at his own joke, he turned, eyes wide as if he'd just heard a sound behind him. "Did you see that?" he asked.

"What?"

"It was like a big blur. A big black blur."

"Our Jacob Marley ghost, eh?"

"No, seriously man. It was like..." He paused,

chewing on his lip.

"Like what?"

"It sort of looked like, well, like a ninja."

"Are you serious?"

"Listen, I know how it sounds."

"I don't know if you do, Gil, because it sounds crazy. I'm beginning to think there is no one in this building except me, you, and the sea monster. I think a ninja would really tip us over the edge of crazy."

Apparently, my words temped fate all too well. Above us, the lights snapped off, dousing the room in a pitch black darkness.

"Watch out, the ninja's around!"

"Be quiet. Where did you put the flashlight?"

"Did I have it?" he asked. "I thought you had it."

I patted down my pockets, as if I could lose track of a five pound steel flashlight. "I must have dropped it."

"Probably when we crashed in. I mean you had it in the hall, right?"

"I think so?"

Thunder rumbled outside as Gil and I lowered onto all fours, searching for the light.

"Do you feel it yet?" he asked.

"Yeah, that's why I'm still crawling around on the floor."

"Ah, yes, okay. Is this it?"

"No, that's my hand."

"Ah, yes, right."

"Hold on, I think I've got it." My hand came to a rest on the cold metal shaft of the flashlight. I sat back on my haunches, lifting it.

Thunder rumbled again, this time accompanied by a flash of brilliant lightning. For a moment, the room exploded in white light.

Standing before us was–for lack of a better word–a ninja.

Really, it was just a slender figure dressed all in black, or at least that's what it looked like in the momentary flash of lightning.

I dropped the flashlight and leapt at the guy. The light clattered to the floor and turned on, casting a long beam across the cluttered space. I hit the ninja in the midsection, and together we toppled over a particularly large mountain of books, rolling down the slope and crashing into a table leg.

Gil was shouting something I couldn't hear over the sound of the ninja's fist slamming against the side of my head. I got a good shot into his side, but he was damn fast.

The flashlight beam found us just as the ninja's knee found my groin. I rolled over as he got up and took off towards a spiral staircase against the wall that led up to the second floor.

I only lost a beat or two before I was back on my feet, groaning and running unsteadily toward the stairwell.

"Up there!" Gil shouted, leading me with the beam of the flashlight. "He's up there!"

I took the steps three at a time, only about a half-dozen paces behind the ninja guy. Gil was running behind us, losing a step with each I gained. Lightning flashed again, illuminating the second floor for a moment. The ninja was losing ground, but I could see where he was heading: a window in a small alcove tucked between a pair of bookcases. He was going to make it to the window before I caught him.

Behind me, Gil had just reached the second level. The beam of his light was behind me, waving across the bookshelves and carpeting as he struggled to catch up.

At the risk of sacrificing a priceless work of academic brilliance, I grabbed a nearby hardback and heaved it, sending it spiraling through the air in the general direction of the ninja. I got lucky–either that or I should've been a major league pitcher–and caught the guy on the back of the head with the spine of the old tome. He stumbled and fell to his knees just before the window.

It was enough time, but just barely. As he started rising, I realized I didn't have the time to catch him, so I caught the next best thing: the adjacent bookshelf. I put my shoulder down and hit it full speed, toppling it into the window and the ninja. Glass shattered, and I heard a muffled *ugghh* as the guy went down like a sack of potatoes beneath an avalanche of hardback books. He did not get up. Out cold, I presumed.

Behind me, Gil's footsteps had stopped, as had the waving of the light. I knelt in the darkness over the man, pulling him free of the books. Behind me, I heard Gil yell something. I heard a dramatic snap of a very old light switch before the chandeliers came back to life.

"Sabra cadabra!" Gil shouted victoriously.

In the full light of the chandelier bulbs, I could see our ninja for the first time. Tall and thin, he was indeed covered head to toe in black, including a face mask revealing only two closed eyes. Probably not a ninja, but not a bad guess on Gil's part. I gave the black cloth mask a pull, revealing the man's face beneath.

Well, I wasn't expecting that. Beneath the mask was a pale-skinned and freckled woman with fire engine red hair. "Huh," I said.

"Hey, I know her!" Gil said from over my shoulder. "She's a bloody thief!"

CHAPTER 5. SHE'S SO COLD

"What are you doing here?" Gil asked for about the sixth time. Apparently his version of interrogation involved asking the same question over and over.

While she was still out cold, I had carried her downstairs. Gil had insisted we at least tie her hands, so I dropped her into a chair, pulled a cord off a very old lamp, and knotted the old rubber-insulated wire around her wrists and through the chair's backrest. Since coming to, she had been very uncooperative.

"What are you doing here?" Gil said again.

A line of blood had run out of her red hair, drying on her forehead in a trickle. Other than that, she looked unhurt. Her eyes were knives, though, and I was starting to feel okay about tying her hands. I'd guess she was about twenty-five, but she had smart eyes that made the cop in me nervous. What's that line in *Jurassic Park*? "When she looks at you, you can see she's working things out."

"What are you doing here?"

"Boss, give it a rest," I said, taking a seat across

from her. I'd cleared a wide space in the center of the book mountains, moving everything out of her kicking distance.

"Sorry about your head," I said. "If this place had a working fridge, I'd get you some ice."

She took a deep breath and let it out slowly, twisting her wrists behind her back. I could hear the electrical cord creak.

"This is a good knot," she said. "Eagle scout?"

I nodded. "I was also in the military."

She smiled. "Cop?"

"Yep. Cop, too."

She smiled again, this time with less humor and more venom. "You seem too smart to be a cop. Not by much, but just barely."

"Cop jokes don't bother me," I said.

"How about dumb jokes. Do dumb jokes bother you?"

"Not really, no."

"Well, rats. And here I was just gonna make you all Hulk smash so I could escape."

"You're pretty clever."

Gil appeared at my side. "What are you doing here?" he asked.

"That's the wrong question, Boss. The better question is what book were you looking for?"

A faint line appeared at her brow. Surprise. "What?"

"You're in a creepy mansion hospital in the

middle of the night, and rather than trying to lift antiques or medical relics–or just escape with your life, we'll get to that later–you're in the *library*. I don't think you're responsible for this whole mess of books, but you're probably responsible for at least some of it. When a thief is in a library in the middle of the night, it's usually not because they're looking for a good read. You're looking for something worth money, and if you're in a library then it's a book. So, what book were you looking for?"

Back to the silent treatment. I turned to Gil. "What's her name?"

"Jane Julius," he said. "I caught her one time in my penthouse of all places, trying to steal a painting. A painting of all things! I mean, why bother?"

"It is a priceless relic, you old fool," she growled.

"What'd I say about being mean?" I said. "No name-calling. If you aren't gonna make me mad, you *really* aren't gonna make him mad."

Gil smiled and stuck his tongue out.

"So what book was it?"

Her gaze moved slowly from Gil to me. I didn't like looking into her eyes. They were like a hungry lion's.

"How much do you know about this place?" she asked.

"A little. You?"

"More than you, I'm sure. I've been researching this place for weeks. I've read enough about it to make me surprised to find someone else here."

"Why?"

A different crease on her brow. Confusion, this time. "What exactly *did* you read about Callowleigh?" she asked.

"Um, well. Opened at the end of World War II as a site of surgical recuperation and rehabilitation. It functioned mainly as a sanatorium for veterans until it was forced to close in the late fifties due to..." I glanced at Gil, wishing he'd read something. Or anything at all. I didn't understand the full implications of what I'd read, and I knew he would. I was a little uncomfortable admitting how little I understood to the girl. It was like being called on in high school when you didn't *really* know the answer. "Due to mysterious deaths. Lawsuits were raised–"

"That's it?"

"What?"

"That's all you know?"

"I mean, I know people died here, which would explain the whole haunted thing."

Gil spoke up for the first time. "What kind of deaths, though?"

"I, well, I couldn't find many details, honestly. I think the lawsuits kind of buttoned them up for good." Gil bit his lip and looked down at the floor.

It looked like he was thinking, after a moment I realized he was looking at the books at his feet.

"What?"

Jane smiled. "Abercrombie knows there's more to this," she said.

"It's not a haunted mansion hospital thing," he said. "It's... worse."

"Yes, it is," she said.

"Do you remember when I told you that books could be very dangerous things?" he said. "That there is a reason that libraries have guardians."

"I mean, I remember you saying it, but you didn't exactly elaborate."

He dug his toe into the pile of books on the floor and turned over a few copies. "I need my pipe," he said finally. "I need to think."

"Boss?"

He raised a finger. With his other hand he pulled his pipe from his jacket once again and began packing it with tobacco. I gave him a minute, understanding that Gil's walking encyclopedia–Finch–wasn't here. He knew most of what Finch knew, it just took him a lot longer to recall.

Jane looked at me, pouting her lips, and smiled alluringly. "Hey," she said. "Hey, why don't you come over here, big fella?"

I gave her a look of genuine confusion. "Why would I do that?"

"Well, you look like you appreciate a good–"

"Why don't you stop right there." I couldn't

help but smile. "We're here trying to rescue a missing caretaker and you're here to loot the place. I wouldn't call that 'together,' would you? Now you're trying to seduce me? While you're tied to a chair? Seriously?"

She sighed, her countenance hardening in the blink of an eye. "If this caretaker of yours is still alive–and I'm not saying one way or the other, quite simply I don't know–then he is only the fourth living *human* in this whole place. The other three are all in this room."

"What's your point?"

"We should stick together. Just because we're the only three humans alive in this room, doesn't mean we're the only things alive in this room."

"This is a library," I said. "The only things in here are us and books."

"That's right."

"So? What's your point?"

"Some books are very, very dangerous," Gil interrupted. "And some books are... well, for lack of a better word, alive."

"Alive?"

Jane smiled. "Yes, alive."

"I... don't think I follow."

Gil sighed. "This is Finch's thing, and I wish he could explain it to you, but some books are tied to this world through their history. Sorry if I get too abstract here, but it is written that the only true history is that which is written in blood. I'm not talking literally, but rather history that is created by *spilled* blood. You know, like wars and assassinations and martyrs. Anyway, unlike simple ink, blood can't be so easily erased. Or forgotten. Ergo, history created by spilled blood ties the written words to the lives lost."

"Hold on," I said. "The big guy's not really following. I'm the brawn, remember?"

"Okay. Try this on for size: you've heard 'the pen is mightier than the sword,' right?"

"Of course."

"The philosophy behind the expression is that words can be more dangerous than weapons."

"Sure."

"Well, I imagine you would agree that just as many people have died because of beliefs or ideologies or doctrines or contracts or treatises as have died in wars?"

"I dunno, I guess."

"Okay, well stick with me here and try this idea on for size, it's the crux of the argument. Some books gain power through the lives that are lost because of them. Following me?"

"You mean people who have either sacrificed themselves or been killed because they believed in or ascribed to a specific text?"

"Exactly."

"That can give a text power?"

"In the same way that true and genuine belief can, yes."

"And so some books..."

"Some books are *very* powerful. Powerful to the point of being dangerous because of the amount of passionate blood that has been spilled either because of them or in their name."

"And some of these books..."

Jane spoke up. "Some of these books are in this very room," she said.

"What I can't figure out," Gil said, "is *why?*"

"Because of a man named Deacons Fehr," Jane said. "He was a Dutch doctor who worked here in Callowleigh from the day they opened to the day they closed."

"I don't know that name," Gil said. "Who is he?"

The girl smiled. "I don't work for you, Mr. Abercrombie, and so I don't particularly feel compelled to cooperate." She sat back, grinning smugly. "But I'll give you a hint."

He raised his eyebrows. "Oh?"

She nodded. "*Y Ddraig Goch*," she said in a whisper.

Gil's eyes widened. "Are you serious?"

Her mouth fell open in shock. It was immediately apparent she had never expected him to recognize the words she'd spoken. "Wait, do not say anything more. I shouldn't have, do not speak its name aloud–"

Gil's hand smacked his forehead. *"Y Ddraig Goch? The Red Dragon? The Sworn Book of*

Honorius?"

Jane was hissing wildly now, her body shaking against her bindings and the chair. "Silence, you fool! *Be silent!*"

But Gil was lost in some revelation. *"Le Veritable Dragon Rouge? Good grief! The freaking Grand Grimoire?"*

Above us was a popping. Collectively, we turned our heads to the cathedral ceilings in time to see chandeliers swinging, their lightbulbs exploding. It started at the rear of the room and moved towards us like a lit fuse, leaving nothing but darkness in its wake.

"You moron! You complete idiot! You do not speak its name! It is *listening!"*

"What?"

The doors to the library opened in a gust of ice cold air before slamming shut. They had no trouble latching and locking this time. Above us, the last lightbulb exploded, leaving the entire room lost in pitch black.

"Oh crap," Gil muttered. "We're trapped."

Around us, we could hear noises, subtle at first but not for long. It sounded like pages turning. Then came the *hiss* of snakes. Then came the sound of footsteps. Big ones.

CHAPTER 6. HOLD ON TO YOUR HAT

Before anyone could speak, I was on one knee, untying Jane's hands by memory.

"Shit man where's the flashlight?" Gil squeaked. "I thought it was right here..."

"Get up," I said, pulling the cord away and throwing it aside.

Jane was on her feet in a second, turning to face the sound. It seemed to be coming from the direction of the library's main entrance.

"Got it," Gil said, the flashlight clicking to life.

"Up, we must go *up*," Jane said. Like a shadow, she disappeared. I grabbed Gil's arm and pulled him after me as I struggled to follow the girl.

I got to the spiral staircase before Gil. The floor around me was coming alive to the sound of snake rattles. "Boss, let's move."

Gil arrived a few paces behind me. I took his arm and guided him up the steps. From above us, I could hear Jane's voice. "Get that ogre up here to help me clear the window! There's no other way out."

"He's coming," Gil panted.

On the mezzanine, Jane led me to the alcove I'd blockaded with the bookshelf earlier. The wood had splintered, but the case had not totally collapsed. It was wedged into the small nook, blocking the broken window.

"Clear it off," I said as I began tumbling the remaining books off the shelf. "Even I can't move this thing if it's this full."

The books piled on my feet, Gil and Jane pulling them from the case as fast as their hands could move. I slipped my hands beneath now-empty shelves and lifted, muscles straining. I heard wood cracking and felt books fall past my head. I grunted, releasing the case. "More," I said. "More have to come off."

Like I said, I'm a big guy, but even I couldn't lift a six foot wide, eleven foot high mahogany bookcase that was half-filled with books. Gil balanced himself on another case, resting his other foot in my hand, and together we lifted him to the higher reaches of the case. Jane climbed the case like a ladder, pulling books free as she went.

Thunder rumbled, and beneath my feet I felt the entire mezzanine level vibrate with a heavy impact. Footsteps, and they were getting closer. Much to my chagrin, I was right. They were *damn* big.

"Do you guys feel that?"

Gil looked down at me. "Unfortunately."

"What is it?" Jane asked.

Lightning struck, illuminating the second floor. At the far end of the mezzanine level near the back of the library, I saw a pure white, lumbering shape. Lightning flashed again. It was at least seven feet tall, skin as flawless as ivory, broad black wings sprouting from its back and hanging at its sides like two great open claws. Speaking of claws, the pair it had were doozies.

"Shit, do you see that?" I asked, pointing.

Without lightning, the mezzanine was dark. The flashlight lay on the ground by my feet, Gil abandoning it when he chose to climb the case with Jane.

"See what?"

Lightning flashed once more. The monster was closer, the distance between us a mere forty feet or so. If we had one thing working in our favor, it was that the creature didn't seem to be in a hurry. It walked with slow and steady surety, apparently in no rush to kill us.

"Whoa, ugly!" Gil said, tumbling off his perch and crashing to the floor. "Is that what I think it is?"

Jane leapt deftly to the ground beside me. "It can't be," she murmured.

"What is it?" I asked.

"Gotta be Sumerian," Gil said breathlessly. "When you see something like that, you know it's *gotta* be Sumerian. Those Sumerians and Akkadians and Babylonians, man, they didn't mess around."

"You're right this time, old man," Jane

muttered, taking an unconscious step back. "It's a Galla, a demon of death cursed to guard the Sumerian underworld, Irkalla."

"Demon of death," Gil gibbered. "Don't see many demons of birthday parties or water balloons anymore these days. Always death and pestilence and destruction!" He bit down on his lip, grabbed one end of the bookcase, and pulled, the wood scraping across the plaster molding of the wall stubbornly. I grabbed the other side and pulled with him. It moved, but not enough.

"Care to lend a hand, dear? We are all in this together, right?"

Jane put her hands beside mine and pulled along with us. The case moved again. I looked back to our right as lightning flashed again. The Galla was closer, maybe thirty feet. This time, I was lucky enough to see the beast's face. It had the head of a bull, twisted horns rising and curving over its head. Its chest was a knot of muscles and scars. A ring hung from the beast's nostrils.

"Must go faster, lady and gent!" Gil said, grabbing and pulling once more.

I raised my leg and dropped it, smashing through a shelf with a *crack*. I raised it higher and broke another. When the shelves rose too high for my leg, I put my two big hands together to form one bigger fist and swung. If we couldn't move the case, we'd go through it.

The wood splintered and fell to pieces easier than I'd hoped, and together Gil and Jane helped me literally pull the case apart. With the case in ruins, Jane slipped through the newly opened window and disappeared outside.

"Up you go, Boss," I said, giving Gil a leg up, conscious of the fact that the Galla was *maybe* fifteen feet away. Maybe.

Gil disappeared out the window. Outside, I heard him bickering with Jane. I grabbed the frame, lifting myself up and out, but not before I picked up a sturdy piece of timber, complete with a long, crooked wood screw sticking out of it.

Outside, it was raining harder than I'd expected. We were all three on a small landing just outside the window, probably the kind of thing that was meant for a large flower box. Not meant for three adult-sized people.

"We gotta move," I said, peering back down through the window and expecting to see the winged bull any second.

"Move where?" Jane said bitterly. "My ladder fell."

I peered down the roof, seeing a long metal ladder lying across the lawn. It seemed a long way down.

"What floor are we on?" I asked.

"Callowleigh sits on a big steep hill," Gil said, shouting over the storm. "On this side of the building we're up pretty high."

"And we can't cross the roof," Jane said.

"Why not?"

"It's slate," Gil said, pointing.

"And it's goddamn pouring rain," Jane finished.

I squeezed between the two naysayers and tentatively laid one boot down on the rooftop. As I shifted my weight to the foot, my boot slipped. I sputtered something as I lost my balance. Gil caught me before I pitched straight off the roof.

"Yes, it's slick," I agreed. "So what's next, Boss?"

"Up," Jane said, pointing. "We can use the peak of this window and leverage our way up onto the peak of this section of the roof. Moving along the top will be easier."

"For fuck's sake, why?" Gil demanded.

"Worst case you can put one leg on one side and one leg on the other, right?" I said.

"Right."

"There's got to be a way *down,*" Gil pleaded.

His doubt evaporated when the Galla closed one huge claw over Gil's ankle. I lowered the mahogany plank and buried all five inches of the wood screw into the thing's forearm.

"Up!" Gil said. "Definitely up!"

Jane went first, spidering her way up and over the peak without a problem. I helped Gil get a grip before getting a foothold myself.

Jane had reached the absolute peak of the roof and was hauling Gil up after her when the Galla broke free of the window completely and stepped onto the roof with a pair of hoofed feet. I was balanced on the window's peak, board in one hand, one of Gil's big white orthopedic sneakers in the other. I turned in time to see two meaty forearms moving towards my throat.

I gave Gil a last push before I turned and swung the board.

The Galla nearly caught it in one hand. Nearly. Unfortunately for the beast, however, it didn't. The board broke across the Galla's bull jaw, tipping it backwards as thunder crashed.

"Dylan, give me your hand, man!"

I turned to see Gil reaching for me. He and Jane were on the peak, Jane holding his soaking wet tweed coat and leaning back to counterbalance Gil as he leaned towards me. I reached up.

Apparently, the bull had a hell of a jaw. My fingers were just inches from meeting Gil's when the Galla wrapped two tree-limb-sized arms around me and lifted me with a *swoop* of its massive wings. I felt the crush of its strength just before my feet left the wet slate surface of the roof and it lifted me up into the air.

CHAPTER 7. ALL THE WAY DOWN

"Holy cow!" I heard Gil shout as I passed over his head. His hands may have touched the soles of my boots as they flew past.

I hadn't dropped what remained of the bookshelf plank, but I'd lost at least eight inches or so from it when I'd cracked it on the Galla's face. With my arms pinned at my side, I didn't have much room to repeat, but unless I could convince the demon that putting me down was wise, I was gonna need to give the thing some other incentive to drop me.

The Galla was carrying me over the length of the roof, through sheets of intensifying rain and gales of wind. From my new vantage, I could finally see the scale of the old sanatorium.

At one point, it may have been a mansion, but multiple buildings had been added over the years, growing the structure and giving it a real Frankenstein look. Roofs of different heights rose and fell across Callowleigh's profile. The Galla looked to be carrying me back toward the main building at the center of the complex.

In my right hand, I spun the shard of wood so it was jagged edge downward. My back was smushed up against the Galla's chest–real up close and personal. Close enough to feel it breathe, hot exhales blowing across my neck.

I twisted, trying to gain some leeway to move. I flicked rainwater from my eyes and looked down on the slate roof beneath as it picked up speed. I shifted, catching a glimpse of Gil and Jane far below me, running precariously on the peak of the roof, shadowing the Galla and it's baggage–me.

"Hold on, big man!" Gil shouted, his voice cracking like a teenager's.

With every ounce of muscle I could manage, I leaned downward, pushing all my weight onto the wood and jamming the jagged edge straight into the demon's leg.

The monster snorted, clacking its jaws and roaring as its wings sputtered and we lost speed. I pushed harder, twisting the wood deeper and feeling hot blood squirt over my hand. The demon's body writhed and we lost more speed, its wings flapping with alarming irregularity. We lost altitude. Then a little more. I struggled against the Galla's iron grip. Pushing once more, I felt its grasp loosen as one hand moved towards its bleeding thigh.

I let go of the wood and focused only on escape. I reached up, slapping at the Galla's face as I grabbed for the bull's throat. Dull teeth nipped at my hand. It missed a few times, but caught me at least once, tearing a chunk of skin off my hand and drawing blood. I smacked at the demon's face and lunged once more, this time catching a twisted horn. I pulled, wrenching the bull's neck as we skittered across the sky. With one hand already looking to remove the wood spike, the Galla released its other hand. When the second hand released me, I let go of the horn.

I fell.

We were probably only about fifteen feet above the peak of the roof when the demon dropped me. I was, however, probably about a hundred feet from the ground.

Falling, I saw Gil and Jane, wide-eyed and in shock, break stride and force themselves to a halt. On the wet slate with no traction to speak of, they slid.

I hit the roof just below the peak, and it felt like I had bellyflopped onto a frozen swimming pool. Gil, sliding crazily, was a few feet behind.

I'm not sure if it was the age of the roof or my speed or my weight, but I went through the slate tiles like they were made of construction paper. Gil followed me through the Dylan-shaped hole, arms spinning, and shrieking like a child.

I fell for a few feet before crashing through a folding table and landing unceremoniously on what looked like an old attic floor. I began raising my head, dazed and confused, when Gil landed on my back.

The old dry-rotted planking beneath me

cracked and sagged downward. Gil reached out and laid a hand on the crushed table. Nothing else was within reach.

"Don't move," I muttered. I tasted blood in my mouth and I was pretty sure I split my lip.

"Yeah, I'm thinkin' that's wise," Gil said.

Above us, I heard muted profanity accompanied by the squeaking of rubber-soled shoes. The caboose of the party.

"Oh no, no, no!" Gil said.

I closed my eyes and braced for impact. Nothing. After a long moment, I turned gingerly and glance up at the hole I'd punched through the ceiling.

The black shape of Jane dangled from the edge of the gap in the roof, rainwater trickling down on my face. She had a grasp on the slate tiles and she was trying to pull herself up and back onto the roof. I could see the side of her face, only just. Her jaw was clenched and her whole body was shaking with exertion.

"Slow," I said. "Slow, Jane. You can do this. Just go slow. You can–"

She fell with a faint *fffft* as her gloved hands slid off the roof tiles.

Her body landed on top of us. The attic floor broke beneath our weight and we fell straight down.

We went through a few layers. A sub-ceiling and then a drop ceiling, maybe a thick layering of insulation. Finally we went through what felt like a few couch cushions nailed to cheap particle board. After that, we were inside a room. Unfortunately, it had a high ceiling. When we finally hit the ground, I was still on bottom.

"Good grief," I muttered as the gang clambered slowly off my back. They climbed to their feet without any trouble, and I was jealous. My whole body was screaming.

"You all right, big man?"

"Ugh, I feel like Evil Knievel after a particularly average day." Gil rolled me over and helped drag me back to lean against a wall. It was rather soft. After a moment, I paused, a thought dawning on me.

"Is this wall... padded?"

"Um, yeah."

I opened my eyes but couldn't see much. Rain was pouring through the series of holes above us and pattering to the floor beside me. I couldn't have cared less at the moment. Above us, I could hear thunder rumble.

"Where's the demon?" I moaned.

"After it dropped you, it continued on. I don't anticipate its return," Jane said, her voice cool.

I moaned. My face felt swollen. Hell, my whole body felt swollen. "Is this room...?"

"Yeah," Gil said. "This is a sanatorium, after all."

"It makes sense that in a facility designed for physical and psychological rehabilitation there would be at least one padded room," Jane said.

"What are you doing?" I asked.

"Trying to open this door."

"Locked?"

She sighed, sounding annoyed. "It has six deadbolts."

"I mean, it's a padded room," Gil said.

I leaned back and moaned again. "Totally safe and secure. Hey, the floor's not padded," I muttered, as every square inch of my body served as a throbbing reminder. "Seems like a bit of an oversight. I think I'd like to lodge a complaint with the management."

CHAPTER 8. THE WORST

"Are you gonna tell me about this book thing or what?" I asked.

I was still leaning against the wall in the exact same position I'd been earlier, plugging my bloody nose with bits of wadded cotton I'd made from tearing up a handkerchief Gil had in his coat.

"No," Gil and Jane said in stereo.

"Ah, okay. Great."

Jane was on one knee in front of the door–also padded, by the way–and Gil was seated beside me, playing his Gameboy. When I'd reminded him that we were trapped in a padded room inside a haunted sanatorium while a demon from Hell was searching for us and a sea monster waited below, his only response was, "Playing *Home Alone 2* helps me think. Besides, you got any better ideas?"

The fact was that I didn't have any better ideas. I didn't have any ideas at all. Jane had been working on the locks for a while now and didn't seem to be making much headway. Even if we got out, then what? We were now totally lost, any bearings we'd gotten after entering Callowleigh were scrambled thanks to our little rooftop detour. And after our encounters with the Galla, the pool Kraken, and the fresh blood, I was beginning to doubt the well-being of Mr. Dawkins, something that was only making me feel worse.

So I watched Gil mash buttons and Jane twist her tension wrench in the second lock down from the top, and waited.

At some point, I dozed off to the sound of rain. I awoke to the sound of Jane's voice, which, personally, I found much less relaxing.

"Because I didn't *expect* you to know," she said. She was resting against the door, her lock-pick kit scattered around her.

"Why wouldn't I know? This is my business," Gil said defensively.

"Because *Y Ddraig Goch* isn't exactly on the *New York Times'* bestseller list."

"I know it because it's my job to know things like that."

"You didn't know what you were getting into here."

"That's different."

"Why? I don't think it is," she said. "A little digging around and you would have found that this place is more than just a filthy, condemned hospital."

"This job was a favor, nothing more. When my client tells me it's safe, I take them at their word."

"And you're still alive? How long have you

done this for a living?"

"Hey, master thief, your ass is just as trapped as mine, and you're apparently very well-informed."

That shut her up. She muttered something and went back to picking the lock. Gil sighed and went back to his Gameboy. He was trying to keep his voice low because I'd dozed off, but I could tell he was mad, and Gil didn't get angry often.

He lowered the Gameboy again. "Listen," he said, "I'm sorry. Sorry for playing *my* part in getting us trapped. I won't take all the responsibility, but I'll take some. But now we're stuck and we have to work together."

She ignored him.

"Well?" he asked.

Nothing.

"What about Deacons Fehr?" I asked. Gil turned to me, a faint look of surprise on his face. Jane glanced over her shoulder warily.

"Oh, are you awake, mongo?" she asked.

"You mentioned him in the library, insinuating that he was responsible for... for *that* book being here in the first place."

"He *is* responsible."

"Who is he exactly?"

"He was a doctor," she said. With a sigh of satisfaction, she finished with the third lock, turning it over and pulling back the bolt. Three to go. "He's dead now."

"He worked here?"

"Yes. He was brought on when the place opened and he was here until they closed."

"A regular doctor interested in otherworld medicine, eh?" Gil asked. "I've got somebody like that on my payroll."

"It's more complicated than that," Jane said, moving onto the fourth lock. "He wasn't interested in medicine. He was interested in black arts."

"What did that have to do with this place?" I asked.

Jane looked at me like I was admitting a mental handicap.

"The patients," Gil said softly.

The look I gave them both told them I still wasn't following.

"The worst of the black arts require an exchange for power," Gil said. "Like blood."

"You mean... like sacrifices?"

"An archaic term," Jane said coolly, "but essentially, yes."

"He could have done his work, losing a patient here and there, and it wouldn't have raised any red flags," I said.

"Yes, exactly."

"What about at the end?" I said, starting to connect dots. "How exactly *did* Callowleigh close?"

She stopped working for a second, but didn't turn. "A mass-death. It was labeled a 'quarantined epidemic,' but those who survived knew it was something else."

"Something Fehr did?" Gil asked.

"Most likely," Jane said, turning over the fourth lock. "Anyone who would know for sure is dead."

"Because of this book?"

"We don't speak of the book," Jane said. "It is too dangerous."

"Yeah, yeah, I know," I said. "It's *listening.*"

"Don't mock what you don't understand," she snapped. "That book has killed many people, and it is the only copy on this world. It is very, very powerful."

"What about the Galla? Did the book conjure the Galla."

"That's what I was thinking about," Gil said. "The book could call the Galla, but only when used by another."

"I don't think that's true," Jane said.

"Well, I do, missy. The... well, the *Ddraig Goch* isn't malicious in and of itself. Like most grimoires, it merely exists. How it is used is up to he who controls it."

"Or she," Jane said.

"Whatever, you know what I mean."

She paused. "You may have a point," she said begrudgingly.

"So what are we saying? That someone is in possession of this *Ddraig Goch* thing and is doing all this? They're haunting this place?"

"This place isn't haunted," Gil said. "I kept

thinking it wasn't, and I was right."

"If it's not haunted, what is it?"

"It's a festering sore," Jane said. "Ever since the war ended, Fehr has been using the library to store his amassing collection of grimoires. This place has become a source of dark energy and power that can no longer be ignored."

"And someone has come for the *Ddraig Goch,* with intentions of using it for bad stuff, I assume," Gil said. "I think that's the crux of it, really."

"Yes," Jane said, turning over the fourth lock. "I'm on a roll," she said to herself.

"Okay, dumb question," I said. "What exactly is a grimoire?"

Jane barked a bitter laugh, but added nothing else.

"The short answer is that a grimoire is a book of magic," Gil said. "Sometimes it's all spells or incantations, sometimes it's a secret otherworld history, sometimes it's just directions on how to make things like charms or talismans. 'Grimoire' is really just a blanket term for otherworld texts."

"That is an understatement," Jane said. "They are not to be taken lightly."

"I didn't say they should be taken lightly," Gil said. "I know exactly how dangerous they can be. But like I said, grimoires are not inherently good or evil, they merely contain magic in some form or another. Terms like 'black grimoire' are totally subjective. How they are used is up to he–or she–

who controls it."

"Usually used for evil," Jane muttered.

Gil ignored her. "Remember how I was telling you about how books have power? Well one reason that grimoires are so powerful is that there are usually very few copies of any given grimoire in existence. In fact, in a lot of cases, grimoires exist as single copies only. Either they were only printed once or all other copies have been destroyed. Grimoires have never been printed or maintained on large scales, probably because of their occult status. It is in this way that they differ from other powerful texts, like *The Bible* or *The Qur'an*. Each of those books exists in such mass quantity that their power is really dispersed. If you found a very old copy of *The Bible,* it would be much more formidable, power-wise. A book like *Y Ddraig Goch?* It's like Highlander, man, there's only *one,* so you better believe it's freakin' powerful."

Made sense. "And you can't tell me anything at all about this *Ddraig Goch?"*

Gil looked at Jane, but she was distracted, cursing the stubborn tumblers in the fifth lock.

"Honestly, I don't know much about it. A lot of what surrounds it is pure myth, really, or so I thought. *Y Ddraig Goch* is like a slang nickname for it, I think it means 'the Welsh Dragon,' but I don't know, I'm not friggin' Welsh. *Y Ddraig Goch* has many names, all referring to the same thing– remember all those other things I said in the library? Yeah, those were its real names. The reason we can say *Y Ddraig Goch* is because it's basically an unrelated phrase that's been co-opted just so we can call it *something*. Don't ever say any of those other things I said back in the library. Any of them. They all invoke its power. Just say *Y Ddraig Goch*. Trust me, people in the know will understand what you're talkin' about.

"Anyway, *Y Ddraig Goch* is a particularly black grimoire written to teach how to conjure demons and, more specifically, the Devil himself. Kinda freaky," he said. He clicked off his Gameboy and stuffed it back into his pocket. "For a long time, no one was certain the thing even existed. Finch told me that it dated back to the sixteenth century, but I haven't even gotten a consensus on that." He shook his head. "I've no way of knowing if it's real. Which was why I said it's name," he added defensively under his breath. "I never thought I was going to invoke it in any way. But apparently I did. So I guess it's real. And it's *close.*"

The last bit there seemed to make him uncomfortable. I could tell by the way he was still blushing that he felt sheepish about saying the book's name, and I felt bad for him.

"How were you to know?" I said. "This thing isn't even supposed to be real. And everything you've heard about it may have been myth."

"It was still careless," Jane answered bitterly. "Anyone who knows anything about *Y Ddraig Goch* understands exactly what is at stake."

I started to speak up but Gil stopped me. "No,"

he said. "She's right."

It was hard to argue when you're in over your head, so I conceded.

Jane stood and cracked her knuckles. With a dramatic flourish, the turned the doorknob and pulled the door open.

"All right," she said. "Let's go."

CHAPTER 9. YESTERDAY'S PAPERS

Corridors. I swear, I got enough corridors in Callowleigh to last me a lifetime.

We wandered for what felt like days. In retrospect, it was probably just a couple hours, but at the time it felt unending. As I had seen from above, Callowleigh was a ramshackle architectural mess, buildings growing off of buildings like Frankenstein limbs. Over the years, it had grown continually and seemingly without any order, like the deep root system of a very old tree. Jane, Gil, and I learned this the hard way. We walked down one deserted corridor after another after another.

It was Jane who found it. I was tired and punch-drunk. I think Gil was just tired (and bored). He'd missed a large portion of his *Hercules: The Legendary Journey* marathon and was a little salty about it. Midnight had come and gone.

It was a door, nondescript and unmarked like all the others. You see, we'd checked each and every door—for a while. Most were offices, stripped and empty. The rest were patient examination rooms, also empty. Soon we began to only check doors at the ends of corridors, hoping for a stairwell. We found some. But the door Jane found, placed unassumingly midway down a particularly dark hall, was different.

Inside it looked like a teacher's lounge from a high school. A few desks lined the walls, but the bulk of the space was open. There was a seating area and the hulking shadow of an old refrigerator, now silent. One recently installed bulb was strung from a cord and hung from the center of the room, lit a pale white.

A cot lay open beneath a window with reasonably crisp sheets. On the dust-free glass, fingerprint smudges were evident in the moonlight.

"Dawkins," I said.

"You're damn right, buddy," Gil said, his mind re-engaging.

Jane followed us inside, although her support was less than full-throated. As Gil and I searched the room, she seated herself in an old desk chair and leaned back, crossing her legs with a sigh and closing her eyes.

Beside Dawkins' cot lay his bag. I searched it briefly, finding nothing but dirty clothes and a half-empty shaving kit. I tried not to pause on the fact that it was well after midnight and the old man was not in bed.

"Maybe he got... you know, distracted?" Gil suggested optimistically. "Busy painting a bathroom wall or changing light bulbs?"

I wasn't so sure. On the floor beside the cot was blood, fresh-looking spatters. The white sheets showed a speckling of red dots. I straightened the sheets and found a hole. "Shit," I murmured, "It looks like he may have gotten into some trouble."

Backtracking to the door, I saw blood spatters leading out into the hallway. I followed the trail, but it tapered off and eventually disappeared. It either meant that he'd stopped the bleeding or... Well, let's just assume he stopped the bleeding.

Back in Dawkins' room, Gil had pulled a thick leather-bound book off the shelf. He waved me over, laying the heavy volume down on a desk.

"It's a big friggin' scrapbook thing," Gil said. He licked his finger and turned a page.

Inside were old adhesive pages with plastic covers, the kind of pages typical to photo albums my Mom used to have. There were pictures, but that was far from all.

"What is that?" Jane asked, suddenly standing behind us and struggling to see over my shoulder.

"A life's work," Gil muttered.

That was the only way to describe it, really. Photographs going back to Callowleigh's early, *early* days. The mansion had opened as a hospital in '45, but it had been standing for decades already. The photographs at the beginning of the album started well before then.

The black and white pictures showed the construction of the original structure, brick by brick, from a hole in the ground to the great Victorian mansion that stood at the heart of Callowleigh's huge expanse. It was strange to see how the old place had evolved over the years. Sometime between now and then it had changed from a beautiful house to a horrible, brooding monstrosity of architecture gone wrong. Where the crooked branches struck off from the main structure today, originally a wide porch had circled the house, framed by tall maple trees and deep flower beds filled with what I could only imagine to be bright flowers. Someone who cared greatly for the family and the property had put great effort into maintaining the old album.

We followed the pictures forward through time. When the structure neared completion, people entered the photographs. Men, women, and children–smiles on their faces–began populating the grey images, moving about the grand structure and the grounds with expectant faces of joy. It was hard to fathom how Callowleigh had changed so much.

"Who is this?" Gil asked, tapping a dirty fingernail on the page. "I figure this family is the Callows, right? But who's this joker?"

It was a shadowy figure who moved through the images consistently, unobtrusively even, but consistently nonetheless. Sometimes he appeared out of focus at the rear of a kitchen, behind a mother and child; sometimes he appeared seated on a porch swing, legs crossed, with two young children in the foreground, working in the garden. He was stooped with a slight hunch and a face shrouded by shaggy hair.

"He is in all of the pictures," Jane said softly. "But out of focus or blurry in each. You can't ever see his face."

Gil continued turning pages. He stopped on the first news clipping, the paper yellow with age. Where I had come to expect *USA TODAY* or *NEW YORK TIMES*, the paper read *THE PEACH BOTTOM PICAYUNE*. The date was August 11, 1927. The headline read ***FIRE KILLS CALLOW FAMILY, ONLY MANSION'S LIBRARY SURVIVES***. Gil skimmed down the page before pausing and reading aloud from the article. "'Wednesday's tragic fire seems to have begun on the porch outside the library and spread quickly, soon engulfing the second floor and taking Peach Bottom, Pennsylvania's most prestigious family in their sleep. The remains of Edward, Aileen, Samuel, Sophia, and baby Edna Callow were found inside. Investigators do not suspect foul play. Funeral services will be private.'" Gil paused, chewing his lip. "'Edward, Aileen, Samuel, Sophia, and baby Edna,'" he read again. "Five people."

I shook my head. "Tragic."

"That's not the point, you ape," Jane said, slipping an elbow between me and Gil and firmly wedging herself in front. "Five people," she said. "Abercrombie saw it."

She took over, flipping a few pages back. She stopped at an earlier family portrait taken in front of a pond–the same overgrown lily pond I recognized from earlier. Like the house, it had once been a sight to behold.

"Look," she said, pointing.

"Five people," I muttered, catching up. Five frowning faces stared back at me from the black and white photo.

Gil pointed, reading off the names. "Edward, Aileen, Samuel, Sophia..." he moved a finger back to the pregnant belly of Aileen. "...and baby Edna."

"And our mystery man," I said, adding my own finger to page. The shadowy, blurred figure of the same man was present in the rear of the picture. He was stooped over, apparently tending the garden.

"Staff?" Jane asked.

Gil shrugged. "He doesn't look too old or well-off, so that'd be my guess. Not too tall, even though he is bent over, thin as a rake. Long, shaggy hair. I'd guess he's a teenager. I mean, look at that hair. What a hoodlum." I didn't comment on Gil's own long and shaggy hair.

"He's in so many of the pictures," I said. "If he's not staff and he's not family, what else could he be? A ghost?"

"I told you," Gil said. "I don't think there are any ghosts here. This is different."

"I believe you're right. He's staff," Jane said. After a minute, we continued turning pages.

The photographs continued, now documenting the slow repairs and remodeling that followed the death of the Callow family. The first addition to the mansion erupted off the west end of the house one day. Soon a second followed suit, moving to the east. Slowly, the building grew. Slowly, it lost what charm had remained.

Gil stopped on another news clipping. "*PEACH BOTTOM PICAYUNE* again," he said. "This one's a little less surprising."

It was a report documenting how the state had publicly announced its purchase of Callowleigh along with renovation plans, originally intending to make it a state hospital. The date was 1938.

Pages turned and the war came. More articles followed, most about beloved young local boys dying overseas. Gil slowed down. Sighing in frustration, Jane took over, flipping past pages of black and white pictures of smiling young men in military uniform. I tried to read the names and dates beneath each but Jane moved too quickly.

"Stop," Gil said, catching her wrist. He flipped back a page. "Look."

CALLOWLEIGH TO BECOME SANATORIUM, CALLOW MEMORIAL LIBRARY TO BE DEDICATED. The article outlined the state's plans to convert the hospital, nearly ready to open, into a rehab ward in anticipation for the war's end. It was 1944.

"It took six years to renovate this place?" I asked.

Gil shook his head. "Well, they were in a

depression and all. A war, too. But that still doesn't sound quite right," he said. He traced a finger down the article. "Look," he said. "'Staff is grateful to see Callowleigh reopen after years of unfortunate setbacks.'" he turned the page, but the article was truncated. "Nothing else."

"'Setbacks'?" I asked. He shrugged.

Jane kept flipping pages, her speed increasing.

"This is a waste of time," she muttered, skipping pages in larger sections, her face harsh.

"Wait, damnit," Gil said, reaching to stop her.

"No," she said, and pulled back.

The edge of the heavy leather volume slipped off the desk's edge with a flutter of pages and fell to the floor with a heavy *thud*. The book lay face down on Gil's foot.

"Let me do this, kid," he said.

Jane said, "This is a waste—"

"You know, it's really not," Gil interrupted. "If you want to go look into what you can steal and how much you can sell it for, then go ahead. I'm not here for that. I'm here to find this guy Dawkins and try and save his life. That's it." He knelt and lifted the book with a grunt, laying it open spine-down on the desktop once more. Turning back to the book, he said, "You can do whatever..."

He stopped. After a moment, he leaned forward. Soon, all three of us were bent over the book.

It was a picture of Callowleigh's staff taken on

the main staircase of the sanatorium on the day the institution opened. Row after row of stern, impassive faces stared back at us from the black and white 8 x 10.

"This is 1940-something," Gil said, "and this guy looks like..." he pointed. "Familiar, anyone?"

A shaggy-haired man stood at the back, frowning, his back crooked with an uncommon hunch. Noticeably older, but unmistakable nonetheless.

"That's our man," I said.

"He is young," Jane said. "Are you sure it is the man from the older Callow family photograph?"

"Yeah," Gil said. "It's him, all right."

At the bottom of the page were names listed by row. Gil tapped the page dramatically.

"Well, would ya lookit that," he said.

It read: *Deacons Fehr, physician.*

I opened my mouth to speak and was interrupted by a rusty turn of the room's door-knob.

We three turned as it opened and were met with the sight of the Galla standing, hunched in the doorway.

I know it must be impossible, but I could swear its bull head was smiling.

CHAPTER 10. OH NO, NOT YOU AGAIN

In the pale light of the single bulb hanging over our heads, the thing was even more monstrous than I remembered.

Yeah, it still rippled with muscle. The pale skin of its chest disappeared beneath the thick knotted hair at its waist that continued down its bull legs and to its hoofed feet. More hair sprouted at the hollow of the Galla's neck, covering most of the monster's sneering face like a cowl.

I paused. Something was definitely different. I vividly remembered the creature's flawless alabaster-white skin. The thing standing before us didn't have white skin. It was chartreuse, a sallow and sickly yellowish green. Also, it wasn't flawless. In certain areas, I could see purple lines of varicose veins running beneath the skin like webbing.

"Is this...?" I began.

"A different Galla, yes," Jane said, her voice clinically cold. "There are more than one, you know."

"There are seven and we are one," the Galla said, its voice sounding like a baritone snake's hiss.

"And as one, we are Legion."

Slack-jawed, the three of us took a few steps back together as the Galla folded its wings around its body and took a step into the room, its hoof falling heavily enough that I could feel the impact in my bones.

A fluttering behind us pulled Gil's stuttering attention. "Oh. Um. Shit. Guys? I found the other one," he said, his voice low.

I turned to see flapping wings. The white Galla was crouched on the window ledge, wings moving slowly and steadily, a pair of angry eyes locked on us. A flash of distant lightning lit the lily pad fountain courtyard behind the Galla as its claw hand gave the window a push. Unlocked, it swung open with a creak.

"What now, master thief?" Gil asked. He held the closed book under one arm, eyes searching the room for some kind of weapon. "I figure you're gonna want to open a dialogue? Play some Yahtzee? Maybe braid the hair on their chinny chin chins?"

Jane stepped away from the group and opened a cabinet, then another, quickly rifling through what lay inside. In the third, she found a small cache of medical supplies. Her hands tumbled rolls of gauze and expired meds off the shelf before she stopped. She turned from the cabinet, a smile on her face and a scalpel in her hand, metal edge gleaming.

"I'm all set," she said. "How about you?"

Gil tried the same thing, scrounging cabinets

and drawers with the same dramatic flair as Jane had. He returned with a dented metal coffee pot. He set his jaw and said, "Yeah, I'm all set too, thank you very much."

He handed me something, saying, "Here you go, buddy. Go to town."

It was a fork.

"Oh man," I groaned.

We moved to the center of the room, standing back to back to back, our "weapons" at the ready. Gil had the Callowleigh scrapbook under his arm, the coffee pot held in front of him like a pistol.

"Dump the book, Abercrombie," Jane said. "We'll need every hand."

"We're gonna need this damn book if we hope to understand this Deacons Fehr guy," Gil said. "Why don't you dump your attitude, little lady. That would be nice."

The window behind us exploded. Apparently the Galla had neither the patience nor wherewithal to squeeze through the small opening it had made, so it entered the old-fashioned way. I was facing inward and Gil stood at the back facing the windows. Things moved in slow-motion as I turned to see him raise the book defensively and block his Galla's attack. At the same time, my Galla came at me. I was blindsided.

It was a mistake, obviously. With walls to the east and west and demons to the north and south, we were effectively cornered. I made a mistake I'd made before even though I'd sworn I wouldn't make it again: I assumed that just because something was not human that meant it was inherently dumber than I was. Wrong again, buddy.

The Galla did just what I would have done if our roles were reversed: it attacked the second my attention was diverted. I checked on Gil and got decked by a freight train of muscle and bone.

The demon bowled me backwards and I crashed into Jane and Gil, the three of us toppling like dominoes. I lashed out with the fork as soon as the Galla hit me and I felt the tines rip into tough flesh. The bull jaws opened and came at my face–ready to make me even less attractive–and I had to lever a forearm under the beast's jaw to keep my nose where it was.

Gil shouted as his Galla attacked. I heard the *brrringggg* as the Boss' metal coffee pot hit what could only be the hard bone of a bull's horn. I turned to the sound and caught a claw across my temple. Skin tore and I felt a searing pain. Hot blood ran down my face and into one eye. With my good eye, I saw the claw rise again.

A gleam of metal in the light and a blur as Jane's scalpel swiped through the air, cutting straight across the Galla's face. The monster roared and pulled back as I felt more blood splash against my face. The fact that it wasn't my blood this time was a little comfort, but not much.

"Thanks," I said as I stumbled to my feet in time to turn and see the white Galla's clawed hand slashing toward's Gil's face like a hammer to an anvil. He dropped the coffee pot and raised the thick scrapbook with two hands, meeting the talons head-on. The claws hit the leather cover and sliced into it with a muted *thump,* pushing Gil back a few steps. He readjusted his grasp and twisted the book, pulling the white Galla unsteadily from side to side.

I wiped the blood from my eye and turned my attention back to the Galla behind me. The beast was rising to its feet slowly, blood still pouring from a slice across its face. When it lowered its hand, I saw that its nose had been sliced nearly in two by Jane's scalpel, the dark flesh hanging and blood running freely. It shook its head from side to side once, sending droplets of blood flying.

It was disoriented, I realized, probably not used to getting much resistance from a couple of boring mortals. If ever I was going to have a chance to get the upper hand on a demonic Babylonian hellspawn with only a piece of kitchen cutlery, this was it. I charged.

I was about two or three steps from putting the piece of silver straight through the bull's eye (hah!) when something heavy clocked me in the back of the head. Stars exploded across my field of vision and I nearly toppled over. Stumbling, I lowered my hands and nearly collapsed. I reached out, searching for something to rest my weight on.

It was the book–the goddamned Callowleigh scrapbook–that had hit me. Gil's eyes followed its arc across the room after the Galla pulled it from his hands and tossed it at my head. Apparently Gil using it as a shield wasn't the *best* idea.

After it hit me, it skittered across the floor, pages flipping madly before falling open near the far wall. Gil followed shortly after, the Galla tossing him like a beanbag into the melee.

He hit the dangling light bulb and sent it swinging, causing the light to cast crazy dancing shadows across the room as Gil crashed into the wall beside the book. Jane withdrew from the nearby Galla, shifting the scalpel from one hand to the other.

"Dylan," she said. "You still with me?"

I backed up, the pair of Gallas focusing on Jane and I, apparently ignoring Gil, who looked to be out cold.

"Vaguely," I said. I still felt dizzy, but the stars were fading.

"Get it together," she said.

"I'm not too sure what our play here is going to be," I said, my brain clearing a little. "Can't get to the door, can't get to the window. Can't even get to Boss and the book," I nodded my head in Gil's direction. Her eyes turned to him.

She looked at him, then the open book lying on the floor. Her eyes narrowed and her neck craned to the right as she struggled to read the pages from a distance.

"Move towards that," she said.

"What? The book? A minute ago you wanted

to—"

"Shut up and MOVE!" she said, lashing out at the closest Galla with the scalpel and pushing back against me.

My Galla had recovered, and I suddenly felt like a poorly equipped matador as the winged bull charged me. Against the wall to my left was a small end table cluttered with old, faded patient forms. I grabbed it and lifted it, bracing it against my chest and holding it between me and the Galla.

Its horns punctured through the tabletop and pushed me back a few paces, flattening me against the wall. I raised my hands, pushing the bull's head upward, and planted a steel-toed boot right into the demon's crotch. As per my luck, it didn't do anything but elicit a thunderous punch right back, straight to my stomach. If I'd had good abs, I probably only would have been hobbled. Seeing as I had *no* abs anymore, it was a little worse. I doubled over, releasing the table as all the air flew from my lungs. The bull threw back its head, sending the table up into the ceiling and makeshift light fixture with a crash. With the crash came the *crunch* of glass as the room dropped into darkness.

I collapsed to my hands and knees, retching as I struggled to breathe. Someone was shouting my name, but I couldn't hear them. Finally, I looked up to see Gil jump onto the green Galla's back, a look of terrified giddiness on his face.

More shouting from behind me, Jane this time. I tried again to take a breath and failed. Jane ran past me, her scalpel lashing out, slicing across the green Galla's chest. More blood spurted free. A monstrous fist came up and caught Gil in the face, sending him tumbling off the Galla's back. With Gil and I on the ground, the Galla leveled its gaze on Jane. She squared her shoulders, locking her eyes on the monster's.

That was when things got weird.

Rather than tear her limb from limb, the beast ignored her. Instead, it turned its back to her and snatched the leather-bound scrapbook off the floor with an eager hand. She rushed it as it turned to face her, but was batted aside like a child as the Galla launched off the floor with its two powerful legs and disappeared out the window, its great flapping wings carrying it up into the sky.

From the floor, the other Galla slowly stood, its face a mess of blood. Without a sound, it turned and unceremoniously followed its companion through the shattered window and into the night.

CHAPTER 11. MERCY, MERCY

I took my first breath, and it was heavenly. "What the–"

"It was the book," Jane interrupted, rushing to the window. *"The* book! Did you see it?"

Gil sat up, wiping a sleeve across his bloody nose. "What?"

"Inside the scrapbook you found was a section of the *other* book. Of *Y Ddraig Goch*. I recognized the script. The language, too. I saw it when the scrapbook fell over there," she pointed to the far wall.

"What?" Gil moaned. "How did you...?"

"I've been studying *Y Ddraig Goch* for months, do you not think I would recognize the text when I saw it? Even a fragment of it?" she growled. "At the very least, portions of it are transcribed inside of that book. I am certain."

Gil stood. "So not such a waste of time after all, huh?" he asked. "If you'd given us the time to look through–"

"It didn't matter at the time," she interrupted. "Clearly he did not expect us to find the scrapbook, and when we did, he sent his servants to retrieve it."

"He who?" I asked, still woozy.

"Fehr, of course," Jane said. "Are you paying any attention at all?"

Gil took a breath. "Deacons Fehr. Here in Callowleigh. Well. I mean, it's possible. Yeah, okay, it does make some sense."

"Wouldn't he be like..." I tried to do math in my head. "A hundred years old?"

"You already know that aging and mortality are far more complicated than you originally believed," Gil said. "It is quite easy, especially for someone well-versed in the dark arts."

"Prolonging your life, invincibility, nigh immortality, reincarnation, and bringing the dead back to life, are all possible with use of the dark arts," Jane said with a disapproving look on her face. "In fact, that's just the beginning."

"All right, some of that I knew, some I didn't. But could Fehr do it with this book you're talking about?" I asked.

"He could do nearly anything with *Y Ddraig Goch,*" Gil said.

"Yes, that's correct. *Y Ddraig Goch* would make most things possible. It is clear that Fehr has returned to Callowleigh for the book."

"Why?" I asked. "If he's been alive this whole time, why is he only coming for it now?"

"The impetus of an insane mind is not for us to fathom," Jane said.

"You could just say 'I don't know,'" Gil said.

"Why do you think he's insane?" I asked.

"Because he believes he can harness the power of *Y Ddraig Goch*. Any mortal who believes that is possible must be insane."

A silence fell. Jane paced about the room like a caged lion. Gil rose to his feet and chewed on his fingernails. I was still on the floor, generally dazed and confused. It had been a rough night. We sat quietly, letting words sink in.

"Why are you here, Jane?" Gil asked finally.

She did not stop pacing, nor did she answer.

"You are a known thief," he said. "But you are only known to dabble in occult artifacts. When I busted you at my penthouse, you were stealing a painting, just a regular old painting. I read the police reports on you, paintings and sculptures, they're your thing. Art stuff, but that's it. I mean occult stuff is lucrative, but it's a niche market, and you're pretty successful already. You don't need this trouble. So why are you here?"

She stopped. "Why do you ask, Abercrombie?"

"You're very well-informed for being so out of your depth," he said.

"It's just job-related research," she said. "You can learn as much about Callowleigh with a few internet searches."

"I understand that, and having done your relevant research–for *months*, as you said–you have learned a whole bunch, but not just about

Callowleigh. You've learned about grimoires, too. Learned a lot, actually. Eighteen months ago you probably didn't know jack shit about grimoires."

Her eyes narrowed and her hands curled into two small fists. For the second time that night, she realized that she'd spoken too much, her arrogance showing her hand.

"You're here to steal it, aren't you?" he asked. "The *Ddraig Goch,* that is. I don't know how I was so dense. As you yourself said, it's not like it's on the *New York Times'* Bestseller list."

Jane took a deep breath and calmed herself, after a minute sitting on the edge of a desk. I could see she was weighing her options. "Yes," she said finally. "I am here to steal *Y Ddraig Goch* and there is nothing you can do to stop me."

"Honestly? I don't care if you steal it," Gil said. "Go ahead, take it and put it in a shadow box over your toilet. My only concern is who's paying you to steal it."

"What makes you think I'm not stealing it for myself?"

"You've already said about six times that this is a job," I said.

"Yeah." She smiled grimly. "It is a job."

"Well, for who?" Gil asked.

"For whom," she corrected.

"Who wants the goddamn book, Jane?" Gil persisted.

She folded her hands in her lap and studied her

shoes for a long moment. Outside, the rain started falling once again.

"Who?" Gil asked again.

"I don't know," she admitted stubbornly. "I was commissioned and paid to steal it. When you receive a check as large as I received, you don't ask questions. I've been pursuing it for five months, chasing rumors and legends all around the world. All communications with my employer have been via email."

Gil squeezed the bridge of his nose and closed his eyes. "And now you're here? Let's for a moment set aside me making fun of *your* stupidity for stealing such a powerful grimoire for who knows who, and I'll settle for an honest answer to this question: what information brought you to this scary old hospital in the middle of nowhere?"

She crossed her arms over her chest. "The story... it's strange," she said softly.

"Try me," Gil said. Despite his bloody nose and obvious fatigue, a hint of a smile touched the corner of his mouth.

"I was at a hotel in Prague, finishing a twelve-day research venture at the Strahov Monastery Library, when I received a telegram of all things, can you believe it? I didn't think there *were* telegrams anymore. Anonymous. It said..." she trailed off, searching her pockets. After a moment she pulled a folded piece of crinkled paper from her pocket. She opened it and read, "'You search ends in Callowleigh. Peach Bottom, Pennsylvania, USA.'

Anonymous telegrams sent to Czech hotels in the middle of the night. It's ridiculous. Sounds like a spy film."

Gil reached out and she handed him the telegram.

"This isn't a telegram," he said. "Do you see this?" he turned the paper to face her.

"It says Telex."

"A Telex is like an electrical telegraph," he said. "Not super old, but old enough to have been sent from here. I mean literally from here. From Callowleigh. Old hospitals and sanatoriums would customarily have some kind of long distance communication, especially if they were isolated, as Callowleigh was."

"What are you saying?" she asked.

"If I had to guess?" Gil chewed his lip. "We both know that blood is required to catalyze much black magic, right?"

She nodded.

"Well, did you know that the type of blood is often just as important? Types O+ versus AB- or whatever."

"Yes," she said.

"Okay, well did you know that guy's blood and lady's blood do different things? I mean, they'll respond differently in certain reactions. As will the combination of a man's and woman's blood and different ratios?"

She paused before shaking her head. "What are

you implying, Abercrombie?"

"Killing two birds with one stone," I said, breaking my silence.

Jane turned to look at me, eyes just a little wider than she would have liked. "What do you mean?"

Gil spoke up. "Fehr is here and he's got his captive caretaker, but whatever he wants to accomplish with *Y Ddraig Goch* can't be done with just Dawkins. So he figures he can get you off his tail and solve his blood problem at the same time."

"Two birds with one stone," I shrugged. "It's what I'd do."

Her mouth hung open for a moment. "You must be joking," she said. "If he is even alive, how could he know that I am searching for the book?"

Gil smiled. "Do you really believe that word of your search wouldn't get back to the book's owner? Old Abercrombian saying: If you start searching for dangerous things, dangerous things will start searching for you," he said.

She turned to me. "And you? Do you believe this theory, as well?"

I shrugged. "It makes sense. And like I said, it's what I'd do. I wouldn't want a well-financed and highly experienced thief on my tail if I was in possession of something as powerful as this book."

She stared off into space. For the first time that evening, she looked frightened.

"So you believe that I am wanted by this Fehr. I

am wanted for my... my blood?"

Gil sighed. "Unfortunately, my dear, I believe we've all stepped in it by coming here tonight."

"What do you mean? Fate?" she asked.

"If this theory's right, this trap doesn't only extend to you, it includes Dylan and me now as well. I'd imagine that Mr. Fehr is positively delighted that we're here tonight. Now all that remains is for us to find him and for fate to play out."

"What's that mean?" I asked.

"Fehr is obviously waiting for us," Gil said. "That's why he didn't just have his Galla goons bring us to him directly. He is... what? Preparing for us? Maybe. And now all that we have to do is find him. If what he wants happens, we're dead and something catastrophic and apocalyptic probably happens, right? And if what *we* want plays out? He's dead and we get to walk out of here and go home." He shrugged. "Fate. Honestly, I would rather it just have been the caretaker, you know? Unfortunately, sometimes it's not the caretaker. Sometimes it's an ageless, demon summoning sorcerer with infinite black magic powers instead."

"Awesome," I muttered.

Jane looked pale. "And now what?" she asked.

Gil smiled. "Now we find him."

CHAPTER 12. HAND OF FATE

It was Jane's idea to head back to the library. As I already said, we were lost, but it wasn't impossible. We used Gil's luck and Jane's sense of direction. She was remarkably more helpful now that we'd made it clear that her life was probably on the line. Theories, but they all seemed to make plenty of sense.

"I didn't make that mess in there," she said.

"What?"

She lead the way, walking with a little CSI flashlight in front of her. "It occurred to me why you immediately believed I was searching for *Y Ddraig Goch*. I don't know why it took as long as it did, but at this point that doesn't matter. But it was the books, wasn't it? The mess in the library?"

Gil nodded. "I figured you'd been digging through the stacks, searching for something. I mean, I never figured it was actually *Y Ddraig Goch* that you were looking for. I mean, that's like Bob Ballard looking for Atlantis. I figured you were just some whacko looking for a signed copy of *The Boxcar Children* #1. I had no idea it was *Y Ddraig*

Goch that you were after."

"But you assumed I had been the person searching the library?"

"Yep, that part's right."

"Well, it wasn't me."

"You know, in retrospect, trashing the place doesn't seem much your style."

Jane shook her head. "No, it is not."

"Then who was it?" Gil asked.

"Logic says Fehr," I said.

"But why would Fehr have to dig around for his own book?" Gil said. "If he was always the mastermind here, why would he not know where his best scary books were hidden?"

"The biggest question for me is: why now? Why is all of this happening now? Fehr's been here for, what? Sixty years? Sixty-five? Why is this happening now?"

"Perhaps my employer is beginning to ruffle feathers," Jane said. "Whoever my employer may be."

"I've got some ideas as to who your employer is," Gil muttered. "But I'm not one to speculate. Just make inappropriate jokes, really. As for the whole why now thing? Most likely it's because our friend Dawkins came in here like a bull in a china shop."

"All right," I said. "Then who rifled through the library?"

No one had an answer for that, the most

obvious being "someone else." There may or may not have been a collective groan at the very idea. In my opinion, four people in Callowleigh, the hell house, was already four people too many.

***

It took us another hour or so and about three-dozen dark corridors to find the library again. By that time, dawn was not far off, and I was starting to feel seriously tired. When Jane pulled open the doors at the back end of the library, my first thought was to curl up on a dusty chaise lounge and go to sleep.

Instead of making just such a suggestion, I said, "Now what?" It sounded wearier than I would have liked.

"We search," Jane said. "Whoever was here found what they were looking for," she said.

"What makes you say that?" I asked.

"Because they stopped looking," Gil said. He pointed at the second floor, lit by the light of the moon. A few cases were untouched, books neatly arranged and in perfect condition. "Those escaped intact," he said.

"Was there a method to the search?" I asked. "I mean, did they start somewhere?"

"We're at the rear entrance now," Jane said. "But given the layout of the compound, I would expect that the search would have begun at the front. Our recent wanderings through the patient wings confirm for me that it's easier to approach the library from the front." She pointed in the general direction of the house's main foyer.

We followed her and her small flashlight. At the library's main entrance, we picked a wall and followed the breadcrumbs of book carnage around the entire first floor. Each case looked wrecked. Without needing to confer, all three of us climbed a set of spiral stairs and began the same process on the second floor. We stopped at the first clean bookcase we found.

"Okay, now what?" I asked.

Jane approached the last bookshelf that had been rifled clean and ran a hand over the books that remained on the shelf. The collection of tomes was old and scarred, most so worn and faded that the words etched into the covers were no longer legible. Every book moved when she touched it, responding correctly to her pressure. Nothing was a lever or knob disguised as a book. Everything seemed pretty kosher.

"You want to take a look at it?" she asked.

I did. I went slower than Jane did, lifting most books up, opening them, flipping through them. I wasn't sure what I was looking for, really, I was just hoping something would jump out at me. Nothing did. The titles seemed pretty innocuous, most involving antiquated therapies and psychological theories, most in reasonably good shape save for a dog-eared page here or there. Nothing had any notes that I saw. Names either. That shred of insidious evidence was nowhere to be found. They just seemed like old books.

When I was finished going over the books on the shelf, I grabbed the wooden fixture itself, giving it a few good pulls and pushes. It didn't budge. As far as I could tell, the wall the shelf rested on was solid as a rock.

"Nothing," I said finally. "Maybe we should keep looking? Maybe they didn't go through the books in order?"

"They did," Jane said stubbornly. "It's what I would do. Anything worth doing is worth doing thoroughly. She rifled half-heartedly through a few of the books piled on the floor before shaking her head with a sigh. "It doesn't make any sense," she said. "Why would they stop here?"

"Because they found what they wanted and took it, of course. But I have an idea," Gil said. "Step back and hold onto your butts. Oh, and kids, don't try this at home."

"Boss, I thought you said–"

Gil looked at me and smiled. "I remember. This is a scary place to tap into any kind of otherworld power, but if we're stuck, we're stuck. I mean, we're trying not to use magic here, but I can't let too much caution be the thing that completely stops me. That just ain't my style."

He rolled up his sleeves and closed his eyes, the broad and bushy mustache on his top lip taking on an air of seriousness (how that's possible, I don't know, but he managed). He stretched his arms straight out in front of him and gave them a shake like a superstitious pitcher prior to taking the mound. With a deep breath, he began.

It started simply (as most strange things do). Gil flattened his two hands and put them together like a praying altar boy before he began rubbing them together. Beneath his mustache, his lips were moving, senselessly at first, but soon words started to form. No words I recognized, mind you, but words nonetheless.

The grains of light began falling from between his hands like snow, radiating a soft white glow as they drifted towards the floor. At my side, Jane took a step back, her hand rising to her mouth. Yep, this was definitely not her comfort zone.

With my limited understanding of otherworld forces–in this case, *magic*–I wasn't 100% sure what Gil was doing, but I understood enough to know that he was building energy in order to do something. What he was going to do, I had no clue, but I knew he was going slowly because using magic in a place as structurally and supernaturally tenuous as Callowleigh was dangerous enough to begin with. Nothing wrong with going slow.

When he spread his hands apart and raised them, the glow coming from his hands was brighter, and even standing behind him, I could feel heat radiating off of his body. Jane took another step back as Gil took a step forward, extending the palms of his hands towards the bookshelf. Almost immediately, the books began reacting. Certain volumes began shaking, wobbling back and forth and vibrating slowly. A few books fell off the shelf harmlessly, others rose slightly off the shelves, vibrations strengthening like they were hooked to an electric current.

One volume rocketed off the shelf, shooting straight away from the wall like it had been fired from a gun, zipping over Gil's shoulder fast enough to make his hair sway in the breeze. A second book followed. Then a third. Gil's hands were beginning to shake from exertion. He clenched his jaw and gasped.

"Boss," I said.

He shook his head, eyes still closed. Another book flew off the shelf. Another.

"Boss," I said again.

"Wait," he said, his voice labored.

A crack ran through one of the shelves and the wood groaned as if a great weight had been laid upon it. A second shelf cracked as the first gave way completely and fell off the case.

"Something's wrong," he said through clenched teeth.

A book on the shelf opened slowly, pages flipping, before coming to a rest on a cross-section of the Earth. The book opened wider and wider before the spine cracked and split. Pages fluttered free before a fire burst to life in the center of the book, soon engulfing it. In a moment, the fire was gone, leaving nothing but a blackened husk on the shelf.

As quickly as it had begun, it was over. Gil collapsed to the floor, the heat and light gone from his hands. I grabbed him before he totally fell to the floor. He was drenched in sweat and short of breath. I turned him and eased his back against the bookshelf. After a moment, he laughed.

"That was... bracing," he said. "Ouch." He raised his hands, palm up, and showed them to me. The skin was a burnished red and hot to the touch. It was as if he'd been burned.

"Are you all right?" I asked.

He nodded, taking a deep breath. "I'm not so good at that," he said after a long pause. "With a little training, I'm sure you'll be able to do that, no sweat. Me on the other hand? I'm too old to do that shit." He barked a laugh. "Especially when it's a bust."

"What do you mean?"

"The book is gone."

"Which book? The *Ddraig Goch*?"

He shook his head. "In this case, the book that gets us deeper into this mansion."

"What do you mean? Deeper?"

Gil and I turned. Jane was standing a good twenty feet away, head peaking out from behind a book case.

"Is that you, Jane?" Gil asked, smiling. "I

forgot to bring my binoculars."

She stepped out from behind the bookshelf and straightened her black shirt self-consciously. "Yes, of course it's me. I've just... I've never seen anything like that."

"It's all right," Gil said. "You can come out."

"Did you say it was all for nothing?" she asked.

He nodded. "Yep."

"So it didn't work?"

"No, it didn't work. I guess after Fehr found the book he was looking for, he used it to open some kind of doorway, in this room or somewhere else in Callowleigh. Unfortunately, he took the book with him. See, I did something like a Reveal Spell, and in addition to this whole place apparently being warded, I got one hell of a kickback from the books that *are* still here, and–"

"I'm sorry to interrupt," Jane said, her voice bearing no regret at all, "Nothing you're saying makes any sense to me, but what about that?" She pointed over the balustrade and down toward the lower level.

"What about what?" Gil asked.

"That," she said again.

Gil turned to me. "Can you take a peek, big man? I'm a little pooped. I'm gonna just sit here and sweat for a minute."

I stood and took a step to the railing. Jane's finger was locked on a spot on the far wall. It was a case against one of Callowleigh's main structural walls left over from the original house, and the bookcases that stood against it had opened like a pair of French doors. A dark greenish glow emanated from within. Draped in the glow was a steep and narrow staircase that led down into darkness.

"So after all that someone just opens it for us? An invitation to the basement," I said. "But from who?"

"From whom," Jane said absently.

With a groan, Gil rose and stood at my side. "That's no moon," he said. "It's a space station." He turned to me with a wink. "Get it?"

CHAPTER 13. IT MUST BE HELL

The stairs led down, down deep below Callowleigh's hundred year-old foundations, and seemed to wind endlessly through jagged rock formations and dark earthen chambers. Jane's flashlight did little to penetrate the terrible darkness that was closing around us.

For the first leg of our trip, it seemed no one breathed, let alone spoke. The roughly hewn stairwell looked hand-cut from the earth a very long time ago. And yet, despite the age, I didn't see any footprints, handprints, or human markings of any kind. For all we knew, no one had been this way since Callowleigh had closed its doors, maybe even earlier than that.

We passed through a few small rooms–functioning as little more than landings connecting stairwells–before we actually came to a manmade room. It was not especially long, nor was it very wide, but it was the first place we'd entered since leaving the library that was bigger than a walk-in closet and seemed to have a defined purpose. It was also the first room that showed any sign of life.

We had seen the light first. It came flickering up the stairwell when we'd gotten within about thirty feet of the room. When we cleared the steps, we saw there were torches mounted on the walls, lit and burning with unnatural, white, smokeless flames, casting a pale light across the expanse of the tiny chamber.

From one end of the room to the other, it was probably twenty feet, but considering I had to stoop to fit in the room, it made me feel claustrophobic.

"It's an office," Jane said.

"How do you know?"

"Look."

A desk sat against one wall. It was clear of clutter, although a few books were scattered across the blotter. Jane picked one up and read to cover aloud. *"The Key of Solomon, The Munich Necromantic Handbook, The Seven Days of Peter de Abano, Three Books of Occult Philoso–"*

"Hold on," Gil interrupted. "No Harry Potter?"

"Y Ddraig Goch isn't here."

"No kidding," Gil chuckled. "Looks more like bait than anything else. Shall we continue?"

The second leg of the trip was worse. Condensation was beginning to form on the walls and ceiling, sending thick droplets of water pattering down occasionally on our heads like a lazy rainfall. The sound of running water had also begun to grow, first little more than a distant *shhhhhh* and soon becoming a muted roar.

"You know," Gil said, "Callowleigh is up on a big hill, so we're really not that deep I don't think. So don't be getting all *Journey to the Center of the Earth* on me here. I don't think we're gonna find dinosaurs at the end of this tunnel."

"Not hell either, huh?" I asked. I meant it as a joke, but a little assurance never hurt anyone.

"I mean, I don't think so?" Gil said. "No guarantees, though. Staircases that spiral into the abyss can lead anywhere, really. Hell, Wal-Mart, Cleveland. You never know."

"Great."

We turned another corner and descended down a final ten feet before coming out on a landing overlooking a roaring snake of a river. The water cut a swath through the rocky earth, passing east to west in front of us before disappearing into a gaping mouth at the far end of the room.

For the first time since our descent, a chamber spared no sense of grandeur. Lit by well-placed torches that burned pure and white, the room was huge, larger than a cathedral and just as darkly ominous. Above us, the ceiling rose at least fifty feet or so, long stalactites hanging down like teeth. Before us, a hand-fashioned stone bridge, flat and smooth and void of railings or guide rails, rose over the roiling river, connecting the tiny rock island on which we stood to another in the center of the room. A second bridge connected that island to a third at the far side of the room. The third rock island, much like our own, had the pale outline of a doorway visible. That island's doorway, unlike ours, was lit by one of the white torches that burned slowly and steadily. The island in the center was nothing more than a bare rock circle in the center of the great subterranean waterway.

"Why do I not like this?" I asked aloud. It was kind of like I was looking out over one of those 1980s American Gladiator obstacle courses, rife with horrible surprises. I was certain no good could come from going forward.

"Shall we?" Jane said, taking a step forward and approaching the smooth slope of the bridge.

"Wait," Gil said. He turned to me. "Big man, what do you feel in here? You've been practicing, what are your senses telling you?"

I had been practicing honing my senses, working long nights repeating exercises with Finch. You can usually *feel* magic like the static charge in the air prior to a thunderstorm, and with enough training you can usually begin to sense it. Gil and Finch had been doing it for years, so for them it was second nature. I was still a bit of a magical rube.

I closed my eyes and tried to reach out with my senses. Finch and I had been working hard to get me up to speed, but recently I was running at about a 50/50 success rate. Not terrible, but not great. With my eyes closed, I tried to process what I was sensing in the room and beyond.

I felt the spray of the fast-moving river kicking against the rocky shoreline. I heard the crackling of the white torches. I felt the damp air that had grown stagnant in the cave for so long. I smelled the mold and mildew that had been growing on the rocks for untold years. I heard Jane's nervous toe-tapping. I smelled Gil as his deodorant failed him.

But that was it. I couldn't feel anything running beneath the surface of it all, invisible to the naked eye.

"I got nothing, Boss," I said.

He smiled uneasily. "Me neither. That's why I'm nervous."

Gil grasped Jane's arm and pulled her back. Slowly, he took the lead, climbing the bridge and stepping out over the first segment of river. The water seemed to bubble and churn angrily as the three of us began walking over the twenty or so feet of bridge, making our way to the small rock island sanctuary that waited in the center of the room.

I saw the first slice of color amid the white foam of the river just before we reached the apex of the bridge, a long, bright sword of color that slipped above the surface of the water for only a split second before disappearing again.

"Gil..." I said.

"I saw it."

"What is it?" Jane asked. She turned to me. Her face stricken. "What did you see?"

"It's all right," I said.

She did her best to smile coolly. It didn't really work. "You wouldn't lie to me, would you Dylan?"

I looked back down into the water. More colors

moving like water snakes in and out of the current.

"Uh, well." I licked my lips and tried to look in control. It didn't work so well. "Boss?" I said. "What are we–"

The tentacle ripped up and out of the water, slamming into the bottom of the stone bridge and knocking all three of us off our feet. Jane, eyes wide, opened her mouth to scream (a very un-Jane thing to do). She didn't get the chance.

A second tentacle rose from the water on the other side of the bridge and closed around her waist, cinching tightly and squeezing the breath from her. It lifted her straight up off the bridge and into the air.

I stumbled to my feet as the ground beneath me cracked and began splitting. Jane's feet were up in the air and kicking, but the tree-trunk sized tentacle was literally squeezing the life out of her. I reached out for her flailing leg, but as the stone beneath me gave way, I literally lost my footing and fell, the bridge breaking into smaller and smaller pieces around me. I scrambled for a fresh foothold or something to grab onto, but there was nothing. I slipped through the crumbling bridge as its center collapsed, nothing but the churning water to catch me.

The water was cold, and I landed on my back, but where there should have been a splash, there was a dull *fwapp* that jarred me and made the bones in my back crack. I opened my eyes as shattered masonry fell over me. I wasn't falling, I was rising.

There was some ground beneath me. I rolled over and saw vermillion skin. I'd landed on the cold and powerful body of the Kraken, and as it rose against the river, I rose with it.

Above me, Gil jumped. Despite having no love or loyalty for the woman, I watched as he threw himself at the mercy of a monster for Jane. He flew off the bridge and wrapped his arms around her legs as the beast lifted the two of them higher up into the air. He scrambled for purchase, one hand on her belt, the second on the thick arm of the sea monster. Jane's eyes were plastered wide, but whatever color remained in her face was nearly gone. Even from where I stood, I could see her lips turning blue. She was suffocating, the strength of the beast too great for her to take even a single gasping breath. The beast was crushing her to death.

The Kraken beneath dipped below the waterline, the river rising up to my knees, then to my waist. I struggled to stay on my feet against the churning current. Crouching, I rested a hand on the arm of the monster to steady myself and put my weight on it. Slowly, I began moving forward towards Gil and Jane. The beast's skin felt like wet rubber, thick and flexible as rows of bones moved just beneath the surface.

"Hold on!" I shouted as I slowed, the tough flesh beneath my feet curving and rising out of the water. I wasn't standing on the beast's body, I was standing on the very base of the tentacle that held Jane and Gil. The further I walked, the unsteadier my footing became. I edged out over the water further, my boots slipping more with each step, until the angle of the arm was so great I could wrap my arms around it like a tree trunk.

Above me, Jane's eyes had closed. Her head rested against her shoulder and her mouth was hanging open. Gil had thrown a leg over the tentacle and was prying at the tentacle, struggling to unwind it from Jane's body.

As soon as I closed my arms around the thick tentacle, it swung downward, dropping the floor out from beneath me as it hammered Gil and Jane down into the water. I didn't lose my grasp, but I slipped further down the arm, all three of us disappearing below the waterline.

I couldn't see anything, and all I heard was the roar of water, but I followed the tentacle further under. The pale light from the torches was gone, everything below the waterline was black. I was lost until my hands found skin. It was Jane. Blindly, I found her waist, my hands closing over the thinnest band of tentacle within grasp. Tiny suction cups on the underside pulled at my fingertips. I closed my thighs around the tentacle and ripped with all my strength.

The fibrous muscle tore in my hands. Somewhere behind me, I heard a terrible bellowing roar as the tentacle began shaking wildly, bucking beneath me like a bull. I tightened my legs and continued tearing.

My stomach lurched as the tentacle rose, the

three of us breaking the waterline and rushing up into the air. Gil was still perched just behind Jane, his hands following mine as we tore into the monster's flesh. Black blood was running freely from jagged wounds. I looked down to see the body of the beast break the surface of the water. The entire creature looked like a huge open hand, palm-up, a team of tentacles writhing around the monster's fleshly body. In the center was a great mouth, filled with row after row of razor-sharp teeth.

We were still rising, a fact that hadn't bothered me until I looked up to see the ceiling approaching and one long stalactite racing towards my face. I twisted, shifting my weight and rotating my body to the underside of the tentacle as a stalactite sliced through the space I'd just vacated before it punctured down into the monster's flesh. That stone was meant for me. Gil wasn't so lucky. He crashed into the flat stone of the ceiling, his head cracking against the rock. His eyes fluttered and his grip loosened.

"Boss!" I reached out and grabbed him as he slipped off the tentacle. Wrapping one arm around his chest, I pulled him towards me, the muscles in my arms and thighs burning with exertion.

I slid, the tentacle now coated with the creature's blood. I lost a few feet, slipping down the tentacle like a sliding board. My stomach twisted again as the tentacle dropped and the three of us plummeted earthward at full speed. I kicked my legs, pulling Gil with me, and leapt off the beast. Together, we fell towards the ground. I carried him with me and we hit the ground in a roll on the room's center island, nearly careening straight off the rocky ground and back into the water.

I dropped him and stumbled to my feet as the tentacle slammed hard into the rocky island. With the impact, something in the monster's grip loosened, because Jane's eyes snapped open and she gasped. The tentacle withdrew and began slithering back slowly towards the water's edge, weak from the deep gouge it had sustained against the stalactite. I grabbed at it, pulling at Jane before it could get her back underwater. More fibrous muscle tore to ribbons in my hands. The beast's grip loosened further, but still not enough. I saw a second tentacle break the water's surface and move towards me.

Magic. Like I said, it's a love/hate relationship. I'd been told I had some in me, an impressive amount even, but my understanding of it was so tenuous that I feared to use it under even the best circumstances. With Gil laying unconscious behind me, I watched as Jane was dragged towards the Kraken's gaping jaws. I didn't have much time to consider circumstances.

I felt the power come from deep down in my gut. It ran through my body like lightning, electrifying every nerve ending and filling me with an endless supply of power. I grabbed the sea monster's tentacle that held Jane and pulled with everything I had.

Veins of power shot from my fingertips where they met the skin of the beast and lanced deep into the monster's flesh like long needles. I set my feet and pulled. From below the surface of the water, the beast rose, huge mouth opening in the pale light and turning to us, tentacles closing in, ready to pull us into its waiting mouth. I didn't let go.

I felt the muscles tear, the tendons snap like taut rubber bands. The skin ripped like wrapping paper. The bones were last. They cracked like huge branches. The entire tentacle ripped free from the monster in my hands in a spray of black blood. The beast shrieked a high and unearthly scream that echoed through the cave and shook dust from the ceiling. I fell backward, the tentacle in my hand, landing in a heap beside Jane at the center of the small island.

The beast, pulsing blood and still shrieking, withdrew. In a wash of black bubbles and vermillion skin, the sea monster disappeared beneath the surface of the river.

I sat up, watching as it slunk away. With a sigh, I collapsed back against the stone ground, eyes staring up at nothing.

Behind me, Jane was sputtering, her breath coming in gasps. I heard a groan, and then Gil's voice. "You all right, little lady?"

The sound of tentacles. Wet and heavy. "Yeah," she said, struggling to get her breath. "Damn, my chest hurts."

"At least you can breathe," Gil said. "Jeez, I'm seein' like three of everything. How many huge gross tentacles are layin' there? Did I hit my head or something?"

"Yeah, against the ceiling," I said. "And there's just one tentacle there."

"Ceiling, huh? Yeah, that'd do it."

"Guys?"

"I'm surprised you're not still out cold, old man," I laughed. "You really got slammed against it."

"Guys?"

"Speak for yourself. I was a big hero, jumpin' on that Kraken like a lady on one of those bull ridin' machines."

"Guys?"

I struggled to get upright. Behind me, Gil said, "What is it, Jane? Can't you let me bleed in peace?"

"Do you see that?"

I turned. It was Deacons Fehr. He was standing on the third island at the base of the last bridge. He was beckoning us.

And he was a ghost.

CHAPTER 14. NO USE IN CRYING

We walked over the last bridge without incident. Gil had a nice bump growing on the back of his head and a fair dose of blood running through his hair, but he was apparently seeing just one of everything again. Jane was walking with a limp, but otherwise she was back to her surly self.

When we reached the island on the far end of the room. Fehr's ghost was gone.

We'd all seen it, nobody could claim it was an illusion. Hell, with Gil's head injury, he'd seen it three times. It didn't help us digest it, though. On one level, things were coming together. On another, nothing was making sense.

"How can a ghost control a grimoire?" Jane asked. "From what I read–"

"You read that ghosts can't harness the power of a sacred text, right? Well that *is* right," Gil said. "Really, it's like an otherworld check and balance. If any old Joe Ghost could use the power of a grimoire, then they'd use it to resurrect themselves. If they could use it to resurrect themselves, we wouldn't have any dead people. Everybody would be looking up grimoire stuff online like Sega Genesis cheat codes and nobody would ever die. Ever." He shrugged. "Clearly that's not the case right now. Unfortunately, we've got lots of dead people."

"So what does that mean, Boss?" I asked.

"One of two things, big man. One? Fehr is really a ghost and he is super powerful. I mean it's weird and unlikely, but nothing's impossible. We can assume that for one reason or another, he *can* use the power of the grimoire and he's behind all this. Two? That specter wasn't real, and it was nothing but a lure to get us to walk across that last bridge."

"There's a third choice, too," Jane said. "And I have no problem being the first of us to speak it aloud: it's possible that there is someone else here in Callowleigh with us."

"Someone Fehr has been working with? Someone alive?"

She nodded. "That is possible, right Abercrombie?"

Gil was silent. His face had taken on a more somber air since Fehr's ghost had made its appearance. The fear that had originally surfaced with the prospect of ghosts had returned.

"Boss?" I asked.

He looked up, apparently not having heard anything. "What?"

We were standing before the doorway cut into

the wall. A white torch in the hall ahead flickered.

Jane sighed. "I said it's possible there is someone else here. If Fehr had a living person helping him, could he use them to channel the book's power?"

Gil's eyes cleared a little, but he was still distracted. "Use them to...? Um. No. No, he couldn't do that."

Jane was skeptical. "What do you mean? Why not?"

Gil ran a hand gingerly through his hair. It came back bloody. "Uh, a ghost can't channel. Not magical energy, at least. They can channel *energy,* but their otherworld magical clout dies with their corporeal bodies. A ghost is literally just a shell. In a spiritual sense, without what amounts to a soul, a ghost cannot channel any otherworld energies."

"Hold on, so what you're saying is that the person channeling everything, drawing all the dark energies and magics from the grimoire can't be Deacons Fehr?" I asked.

He looked up at me. "That's right."

With a little less enthusiasm, Gil took the lead once again, walking past the white torch and into the shadowy hallway. Jane was second. As usual, I was the caboose.

The hall was short, and we emerged on the other side in a dark room lit only by about a million flickering candles. Somewhere in the hallway, the floor had changed from coarse rock to perfectly cut square tiles of granite. The ceiling above us was a well-carved cathedral ceiling that rose in a dome to a point. The main area of the rectangular room was empty, the walls leading to what looked like an altar on a dais against the back wall.

"It's a church," I said.

"This ain't no church," Gil muttered.

Even speaking as softly as we were, our voices carried, echoing endlessly in the room. Soft whispers turned into infinite hushed murmurs. At the front of the room, I saw movement in the shadows. What I'd once believed to be nothing stirred, the flutter of black cloth taking shape in the darkness. The shape turned, throwing back a hood.

It was Dawkins. I recognized him from the picture Eleanor Robbes-Grillet had given us earlier that day. It felt like a lifetime ago.

"Holy friggin' shit!" Gil shouted, pointing. "It's the caretaker! It's the freakin' caretaker!" He turned to me, a jubilant idiot grin on his face. "I told you, man! I told you!"

"What?" Jane and I asked in unison.

He pointed. "Dawkins!"

At the far end of the room, Edward Dawkins began walking towards us, the hard heel of a wingtip tapping on the granite floor. As he approached and my eyes adjusted to the dim light, I saw that he was not happy to see us.

I was a little confused. "No, wait, I thought..."

"Who are you?" Dawkins asked. "What are you

doing here?"

Gil was still not finished. "It's the caretaker! This is just like that episode of *Scooby Doo* about the mansion! And the one about the old zoo! And the one about–"

"Silence!" Dawkins yelled. "Answer me. Who *are* you? And what are you doing here?"

Gil continued to gibber about *Scooby Doo,* so I tried to take point.

"Uh, Mr. Dawkins? We were hired by your employer. Eleanor Robbes-Grillet? She expressed some concern that she hadn't heard from you? Apparently it's been... days, sir."

Dawkins had opened his mouth–presumably to scold us further–when he stopped. "Eleanor? She called me? I mean... Well, you really shouldn't be here." Suddenly very self-conscious of the circumstances, he shuffled in his robe and pulled out a cell phone. The old man squinted at the screen. "Oh damn, there's no signal down here. No wonder she couldn't get through."

There was a silence as Gil and I shared a glance. Finally I said, "What?"

He sighed, all the patience of a very old and very jaded school teacher. "You shouldn't... Oh this is so awkward. See, I must apologize. Had my phone been working, I would have received Eleanor's calls. If I had received Eleanor's calls, you would not have been hired. If you had not been hired, you would not be here in this room right now.

If you were not here in this room right now, you would not have to... well, die. For that I am sorry."

"Hold on," I said, trying to sort things out. "What did you say?"

Dawkins cleared his throat and gestured upwards. "I'm far too busy to entertain, demons to summon, circles of hell to unleash, you see. My friends will have to bid you goodnight for me." He gestured with a wave of his hand.

Gil, Jane, and I looked up. Four Gallas hung suspended in the darkness above us. A marbled grey one and a brick red one joined the aforementioned white and chartreuse. A pretty colorful quartet of hellspawn, really.

"Four?" Gil said. *"Four?* If my Babylonian mythology is correct–and I'd like to think that it is– aren't there supposed to be seven?"

Dawkins sighed and shifted his weight uncomfortably. "I could only manage to summon four out of the seven. That's very respectable–"

Gil nodded. "Oh, of course, of course."

"–I mean, I'm still pretty new at this."

"That's all right," Gil said, throwing a look in my direction. He motioned me with his eyes, but at the time, I must not have been speaking "Abercrombian" so well. Probably because I'd been awake all night in a haunted house.

There was an awkward silence. Well, truth be told, the whole thing was awkward. I looked around for a blunt object or something, anything I could brandish as a weapon. There was nothing, no weapons to speak of. Not even a fork. Gil busied himself by digging around in his pockets and whistling.

Jane, on the other hand, decided to speak. She said, "So do you need my blood or something? How worried should I be? Like, on a personal level?"

"What?" asked Dawkins.

"My blood. You sent the telegram to bring me here. I'm the one looking for the book and so you called me here."

Dawkins squinted at her. "I did not call you here. Although, now that you mention it, your *blood.*" He rubbed one hand on his chin, kicking around ideas he'd never even imagined. "Your *blood,*" he said again. His lips curled back from his yellow teeth. "You know..." He trailed off, weighing his options. Finally, he said, "What the hell. It can't hurt." He looked up into the shadows of the ceiling. "Come legion. Come and fetch me *blood.*"

With the flapping of wings, the four Galla fell from the cathedral ceilings, dive bombing us. Weaponless, we scattered.

Jane and I took off towards the rear of the temple, hitting the deck and moving quickly back towards the hallway and what little shelter it provided. Gil had other plans. Hunched at the waist, he hustled across the room, making a beeline for the altar. Dawkins intercepted him by leaping on his back. The two grey haired men went down in a struggling geriatric heap.

"The book!" Gil groaned as Dawkins put him in a headlock. "Get the *book!*"

I was staying low, but one Galla hit me as it passed overhead, wings flapping. The beast lashed out at me, catching me in the chest with one hoofed foot. I stumbled to all fours as a second Galla landed in front of me.

On the other side of the room, Jane was doing her best to avoid her Galla, which had landed in front of the exit, effectively blocking it. Over my shoulder the last Galla had landed beside Gil and Dawkins. With no effort, it grabbed Gil by the hair and lifted him off of Dawkins, tossing him backwards like a child's toy.

I backpedaled a few steps and rose up, balling my two fists together and swinging them as one. I caught the Galla across the jaw, snapping its head back. I swung again and it caught my two fists in one claw. With a snort, it pulled me towards it and leveled a hoofed kick to my solar plexus, knocking me ass backwards onto the granite. My head snapped back and hit the floor, nice and hard.

Stars. Big bright stars. They filled my field of vision for about the fourth time that evening and my limbs all went numb. When I opened my eyes, I saw two of everything. *Just like Boss,* I thought. *That can't be good.*

The Galla dragged me to the center of the room and dropped me in a pile along with Jane and Gil. I didn't have much fight left in me. None of us did.

From inside his robe, Dawkins pulled a thick

piece of chalk. "Move them aside," he said to the Gallas. "I will draw the runes and summoning circles. We will try the ritual once more." He smiled down at us.

"This time with *blood.*"

CHAPTER 15. ALWAYS SUFFERING

"Well this guy is obviously a big dumb friggin' moron," Gil said. He had another bloody nose. Without anything left to stuff it with, however, he was merely plugging it with the pad of his thumb, his head tilted back.

"No argument, Boss. But how bad is this?"

Gil sighed. "Well, I gotta admit, I would feel pretty stupid if I died at the hands of this jamoke."

"Speak for yourself, Abercrombie," Jane said. "Some of us are actually good at our jobs."

The three of us were lined up firing squad style against one of the temple's walls with the four Gallas staring us down. Dawkins was on his hands and knees in the middle of the floor, drawing all kinds of scrambled runes on the granite.

"How exactly did he summon those things?" I asked.

"With the book," Gil said. "With that *Ddraig Goch,* a monkey could summon the Galla. Hell, a monkey could probably summon all seven." He scoffed, "I mean, it's basically just reading an incantation. The friggin' book does the rest."

"Was that what you were–"

"Gesturing with my eyes? Well yeah, duh. Can't you pick up on the signals? When I go like this," he waggled his eyes, "you're supposed to know I mean 'go that way, grab the magic textbook, and watch out for the crazy wizard guy.' Try to remember that for next time, eh?"

"Yeah, you got it, Boss. So what's our next move again?"

Gil sighed. "I'm workin' on that."

Dawkins straightened up with a groan and pocketed the chalk, wiping his dusty hands across his black robe. "That looks pretty good," he said. He walked back to the altar and lifted a heavy, leather-bound book. He flipped a few pages before stopping. "Ah, here we go." His eyes moved from the floor to the page and back again, surveying his work. "Not bad at all," he said finally.

"So I have to ask," Gil said. "Where did you get it?"

Dawkins raised his head and smiled. "I'm sorry, where did I get what?"

"Your lovely sense of humor."

"What?"

"The book," Gil said. "Where did you get the book?"

Dawkins smiled once again. "It should have been mine all along, you know. I was supposed to have inherited it, just like my mother and father were supposed to have inherited it."

"All right, so who were your father and mother?" Gil asked.

"My father's name was Robert Dawkins." Dawkins smiled. "And my mother's was Eliza Hess, but don't expect to recognize any names. You won't. It's more complicated than my mother and father." He flipped a few more pages and turned his back on us.

"How so?" Gil asked.

Dawkins fetched a handful of other relics off the altar and returned with them resting on the open grimoire in his hands. "Because of what should have happened, not because of what *did* happen. This all should have been mine. Callowleigh, this temple, the library, the books. Do you know how long it took me to get in position to even enter these grounds? *My* grounds? Years. Years upon years." He shook his head and knelt, resting the grimoire on the granite beside him and setting out a smattering of bones across the chalk runes.

"What do you mean?" Gil asked. "Tell me why this should have been yours."

"Was your grandfather's name Abraham? Abraham Hess?" Jane interrupted, breaking her silence.

Dawkins froze, a bone dangling from his fingertips. "What did you say?" he asked.

This time with more confidence. "Your grandfather, his name was Abraham Hess, wasn't it?"

Dawkins rose unsteadily, joints cracking. "How did you know that?"

"Yeah, how *did* you know that?" Gil asked.

"Abercrombie, I told you before: I do my research."

"What do you know of my grandfather?" Dawkins asked angrily. "How do you know that name?"

Jane smiled. "I already said, I did my research before coming here. I know the name Hess because I read pages upon pages about Callowleigh and the town of Peach Bottom before I stepped inside the county. Of course I've heard the name Abraham Hess."

Dawkins took a few steps towards her. "What do you know of him?"

Gil stage-whispered from the side of his mouth. "Uh, yeah. A teeny bit of intel, please..."

"The Callow family was the most well-established, well to-do family in Peach Bottom, Pennsylvania for years and years. Until a fire killed them. The second most well to-do family were the Hesses."

"That's correct," Dawkins said slowly. "Please continue."

"I found unofficial minutes from the inquiry put together looking into the fire. From what I read, prior to the fire it was expected by many that Abraham Hess would marry the young Sophia Callow. Because of that, a few members of the committee named Hess as a suspect following the Callows' untimely deaths. Eventually, he was exonerated because of a lack of hard evidence, although I could find no reason to list him as a suspect at all. Essentially, the marriage would have linked the two most wealthy families in the region. It would have *helped* Hess greatly."

"Yes, it would have," Dawkins bemoaned. "The inquiry almost ruined grandfather, but they had no evidence. There was no evidence left. It was his fault, that terrible servant boy's, that is. That filthy garden boy who ruined everything. He ruined my grandfather's life, ruined my father's life, ruined *my* life. Without that damned boy, Callowleigh would be home. Grandfather would have married Sophia, and all would be as it should. Callowleigh never would have been the awful leper museum it became after the war. The library never would have been forgotten; the books would not have been locked away. Even they would have been mine. But that boy, that little... little *shit* had to ruin it all."

"Little shitboy...?" Gil said.

"Deacons Fehr," I guessed.

"Don't speak his name," Dawkins said, turning to me with fire in his eyes. "Don't you dare say his name in front of me."

"How did he...?" Gil began.

"That Callow girl fell in love with him," Dawkins hissed. "It was a scandal, even then, but those horrible parents wouldn't send the boy away. He was filthy, son of a drunkard, unfit to marry a pig. If they'd only sent him away, away from Sophia, how life would have been *different.*"

I watched him in amazement. It was hard to even fathom the chip still on this guy's shoulder from, what? 90 years ago?

"Who started the fire?" Jane asked.

"It was... It was not supposed to destroy everything," Dawkins sat back, picking his fingernails nervously. "It wasn't even supposed to *kill* everyone. It was supposed to burn *outside* the library, driving the family away from it. Driving them outside. The Callows knew what books they possessed, and they hoarded them. They didn't want anyone else to get them. Once the wedding had been called off, grandfather needed a way to get the books. The fire was not supposed to kill them. It was a distraction, only a distraction. It was supposed to clear the house so the books could be taken."

"Then what happened?" I asked.

"It was a dry season," Dawkins said softly. "Grandfather did not know, he did not understand. The wind came and set the grasses on fire. The grasses burned and the fire spread. It grew. When it was over, they were all dead. The house was locked down and the books sealed inside. The family's legacy was to live on in the library, and all their books were donated to the state and used as a backbone for the sanatorium's library, the Callow Library."

"So much for your grand inheritance," Gil said.

"It was supposed to be mine," Dawkins mewed. "All *mine*. It would have changed my life. I could have been a great man; no, I *would* have been a great man. And I would be *home* right now." He sighed, returning to his knees, returning to spreading the bones across the runes.

"And what happened to Fehr?" I asked.

Dawkins smirked. "Got a measly degree and lobbied for a job here at the hospital. He took over for the Callows, watching over their precious books. He watched them right up until he died, destitute and alone." Dawkins enjoyed the last words, stretching them out with relish.

Dawkins stood, content with the layout of bones and runes that covered much of the temple floor. "Are you ready?" he asked. "Since returning, I have been trying to open a portal to the dark beyond. When it opens, this house will be filled with the incredible power it deserves. The power from below. My Galla servants are just the beginning. Callowleigh, my home, will be great and powerful again, and all shall know my name. Know it and fear it."

Gil sighed. "Okay, so sometimes the caretaker *is* the ageless, demon summoning sorcerer with infinite black magic power."

Dawkins smiled at him and gestured to the white Galla. "The woman," he said. "Bring her to the edge. She will be our bait. We will use her blood." Jane opened her mouth but did not speak as the pale-skinned Galla carried her to the edge of the runes and dropped her like a life-sized chess piece.

Dawkins smiled and focused on the text in his hands. With a deep breath, he began reading. The words meant nothing, but the instant he began speaking, the runes began to move. So did the granite floor, coming to life as if the very surface was boiling.

Ripples spread across the floor, radiating out from the center rune like waves on a pond. The smile on Dawkins face grew. At the center, a pinhole of red light came to life, shooting a bright, powerful beam straight up to the shadowy ceiling. Like a whirlpool, the center of the floor began to sink, slowly broadening with each passing moment. Jane edged back, but her Galla sentinel pushed her to the edge once more. Dawkins kept reading.

"Okay," Gil said. "So this is where we need to throw the Hail Mary pass." He looked at me. "You wanna bum rush the Galla, and I go for the old dude, or vice versa?"

"There's gotta be a better plan that that, Boss."

"Well, okay, maybe you're right. How 'bout we *both* try and bum rush the old dude. All we gotta do is get the book."

"Wait," I said. "Look."

Beyond the edge of the rippling granite, something was rising. Pale and translucent, it grew from the granite like a puff of smoke. Slowly, it began to take shape.

"It's... it's Fehr," I whispered.

Gil's mouth hung open. "That can't... he can't." He shook his head. "He's not powerful enough."

"What do you mean?" I asked.

"He can't *do* anything. What's he here to do? Watch?!"

Fehr stood at full height a few paces behind Dawkins. He took a few slow steps forward, his hands hanging down at his ghostly sides.

"Push him," I said. "Take the book. *Do something!*"

"He can't," Gil said dejectedly. "He can't do anything. He is only a ghost, he's not powerful enough."

"Let's attack the Galla," I said. "Make a rush, cause a distraction..."

Gil's face was pale, his eyes locked on Fehr's ghost. "No," he whispered. "We can't. I can't."

"What? A second ago–"

A belch of fire from the center of the widening gyre interrupted me. Jane gasped and pushed back against her demon babysitter. The portal opening in the floor was growing. Long curved bodies of snakes crawled up the sloping sides and slithered over Jane's feet and across the granite. A flutter escaped the pit, and I saw a flurry of black bats rise into the rafters. Dawkins laughed madly but continued reading.

"Boss," I said. "What's wrong with you? What the hell's going on?"

I turned away from Gil's stricken face,

following his gaze. Fehr was walking slowly away from Dawkins, his ghostly body moving as if weighed down by heavy shackles.

"What's he doing?" I asked. "Not helping! He's *not helping*. Come on, Boss, we need to do something!"

"All right," he said, his eyes blinking as if he'd just awoken from a trance. "All right. On the count of three. Are you ready?"

I nodded.

"One," we said together.

Fehr took a few more steps along the edge of the widening portal. Dawkins laughed again as a three-headed serpent crawled forth from the pit, three finger-like necks twisting around Jane's ankles.

"Two."

Fehr turned, zeroing in on something. I squinted. It was one of the bones that Dawkins had laboriously placed at the outskirts of the portal. It was a tiny small bird's skull, although not just a skull anymore, it was glowing, vibrating with power as it stabilized the portal. Slowly, the distance between Fehr and the bone shortened. With a roar, a manticore leapt up from the depths of the pit, teeth bared.

"Three."

Gil and I charged the nearest two Galla. I knocked mine backwards, but Gil quickly found himself tangled in a storm of wings and talons.

My Galla stumbled backwards and fell with me on top of it. I landed a few good elbows to the jaw before Dawkins' screaming interrupted me.

I turned to see Fehr bending over the small skull, his ghostly form moving in terribly slow motion. I remembered Gil's words, *"He can't, he's not powerful enough"* and prayed he was wrong. All he needed to do was shift the precisely placed skull to unsettle the rune and break the spell's potency.

"Do it, Fehr!" I shouted. "Just move the damned thing!"

He extended one long ghostly finger towards the small bone lying on the floor and paused just inches from it. The old specter closed his eyes.

The moment seemed to last forever.

Then he reached out and inched the bone, overturning it and moving it *just* beyond the edges of the rune on which it lay.

A bright light exploded up from the floor, the portal beginning to waver as it lost its focus. Bolts of lightning belched outward, illuminating the temple in crazy colors as the creatures filling the room began to feel the magnetic pull back from where they came. Jane leapt backwards, kicking snakes from her legs as she fell into the arms of the waiting Galla at her back.

The manticore slid back into the portal first, claws grabbing desperately on the bare granite for some purchase before it slipped down into the portal with a shriek.

Dawkins continued reading, the nonsensical words exploding from his lips as he flipped pages, his eyes wide and watching as his creations were stolen from him.

Fehr collapsed onto the temple floor, his face an equal mix of jubilation and terrible exhaustion. His arms fell at his sides as his weary eyes closed.

I stumbled off the Galla and darted toward Dawkins, my feet careful not to cross the edge of the shrinking portal. Behind me, I heard shouting. I cast a glance over my shoulder in time to see two Gallas abandon Jane and Gil as they took to the air after me.

Snakes writhed in nests and were pulled across the floor in front of me. I leapt over tangled messes of them and ran through a swirling cloud of bats as they were sucked back down into to pit. All the while, Dawkins continued reading, his voice quickening as he watched his terrible future crumble around him. Each passing word grew increasingly desperate.

I ran through Fehr's prone ghost before colliding with Dawkins and sending the old man to the floor. The book skittered out of his hands and slid across the tile to the altar dais. Dawkins turned on me, teeth open savagely, and lashed out at my face, his nails tearing my skin. I hit him once, twice, bloodying his nose and dropping him to the floor. Done with him, I moved on, running past him for the grimoire.

From behind, a Galla hit me full force, knocking me to my knees. Dawkins rose unsteadily to his feet. I looked up to see him stumble past me, arm outstretched towards the book. I don't know how many Gallas were on me, but they'd lost sight of Gil. He streaked past us with Jane close at his heels. Skidding to a stop at the altar, he caught up with Dawkins and jumped on him: geriatric melee part 2. Grabbing a handful of the old man's hair, Gil spun him around and laid him out with a right hook across the jaw. I could hear the *crack* from where I lay under the pile of demons. Dawkins went down and didn't get up.

Even before Dawkins hit the floor, Jane had the book. She knelt, flipping pages feverishly as a Galla rose from off my back and descended upon her. Gil backpedaled, putting his body in front of hers and took the full force of the attack, the Galla throwing him back against the altar with a clattering of relics and candelabras.

I gasped for breath, struggling against the weight that was crushing me, throwing elbows and kicks as best I could. At a certain point, I could see no more, but I heard it when Jane began reading.

The effect was instantaneous. The Gallas on my back began to scream and dissolve, their bodies burning with a heatless fire. Slowly, their combined weights dissipated. Writhing and roaring, the beasts seemed to melt away, leaving only smoldering heaps of ashes and a few bones behind.

When I stood, nothing but smoking ash

tumbled off my scorched clothing. The bull horns stood out prominently among the glowing embers lying on the temple floor. Jane was still reading, but it was only for posterity. Her face was pale and sweaty, but the portal was no more. The floor had returned to, well, being a floor. Chalky ruins and a few scattered relics were all that remained.

Finally, Gil rested a hand on her shoulder, and only then did she stop. She took a long deep breath, then another.

"I think it's over," Gil said. He was huffing and puffing, his nose bleeding freely from both nostrils. At his feet, Dawkins was still out cold and Gil was tearing pieces from the dark robe the older man wore. After a minute, he stuffed the cotton wads up his nose, stemming the bleeding. "Ah, that's better," he said.

I took an uneasy step over to where Fehr lay on the ground. His eyes were closed and his mouth cracked open. I knelt at his side.

"Fehr?" I said softly. "Mr. Fehr can you hear me?"

The ghost opened his eyes. *Yes, I can hear you,* he said in a perfectly audible voice that had not been spoken.

Gil took a few tentative steps towards us. "How did you do that?" he asked softly. "How did you move that relic? It should have been... You should not have been able to do so. It is impossible."

Fehr smiled. *I have been trapped as a ghost for*

so very long, good sir. I have spent these many years of my death preparing for such a moment as this. I could not stop the book last time when Robert Dawkins came for it, and all the patients were killed because of it. I didn't know enough; I didn't understand. But after that, I promised myself it would not happen again. I promised Sophia. Over the years, I studied; I prepared. I waited and I protected the books as I said I would. I promised, you see. Even when I died, I didn't stop. After my death, my power was diminished, but I still vowed I would not stop. Not ever.

He sighed, a fine golden dust escaping from his lips. His ghostly form faded for a moment before returning.

"He is... disappearing," Gil said.

"What?" I asked.

"Ghosts," Gil whispered, "are only energy, and when the energy is used up, nothing remains. When nothing remains, they... they disappear."

It is nearly my time, Fehr said. *Finally. Will you take the books, sirs? Will you protect them? I saw you risk your lives to prevent the gate from opening. You stopped a great evil tonight. Please, tell me: will you take the books and protect them?*

Gil nodded. "I think we can manage that, my friend. Rest your eyes. You are nearly free of this world. Do you know what comes next?"

I will be returned to Sophia in Paradise. As a hero, I pray. I fulfilled my vow. I fulfilled it.

"You did that, my friend," Gil said softly.

With a last sigh, Fehr exhaled the last of himself into the air in a soft golden cloud, his ghostly body fading with it. I closed my eyes. When I opened them, he was gone.

Gil sat back on his haunches. "So he wasn't the one behind it all," he said, smiling sadly. "He spent these years as a ghost watching over the grimoires. I didn't know the Callows were guardians, but it makes sense if Eleanor Robbes-Grillet inherited their property. She is, after all, a guardian herself." He stood with a groan, his joints creaking.

"So Jane, I reckon Fehr's ghost sent your Telex from Callowleigh, not Dawkins. He called you here. You were his last hope. He knew he couldn't last much longer. It was blind luck that we came here tonight at all, big man." Gil laughed sadly. "Had that damn cell phone worked, you woulda been on your own, little lady." He smiled over his shoulder. "Jane?"

She wasn't there. I stood and took a slow lap around the room's darkened corners. When I returned, Gil was seated on the altar, shaking his head.

"She's gone," I said.

He nodded, resigned. "And she took the book."

CHAPTER 16. YOU CAN'T ALWAYS GET WHAT YOU WANT

Gil was sitting in his easy chair, feet propped up on the footrest, a pizza box open across his lap. On the muted big screen TV, Vincent Price was speaking silently to group of frightened people.

It was six thirty in the morning and we'd gotten back to Gil's penthouse only about twenty minutes ago. Outside, the sun was just creeping over the horizon.

"Where did you get a pizza at six AM?"

He took a bite and smiled with his mouth full. "A pizza place is always open somewhere. Want a slice? It's Hawaiian, everybody's favorite."

I grabbed a piece and sat down on the couch. On screen, a fair-haired woman was screaming, hands pressed to her horrified face like Macaulay Culkin in *Home Alone*. I pulled my boots off and rested my feet on the coffee table. I was very tired.

We had waited at Callowleigh's main entrance with Dawkins until the police arrived. Soon after the cops had hauled him away–on a charge of trespassing and vandalism, by the way–a team of men arrived from the payroll of Ms. Eleanor Robbes-Grillet. Armed with banker's boxes and heavy wooden crates, we worked with her team to pack up as many dangerous grimoires as we could find. It turned out to be quite a few. Sufficiently comfortable with the fact that, at the very least, we'd gotten the worst of the worst into the safe hands of the guardians (also known as the city's librarians), we headed back to Gil's penthouse in search of food and sleep.

And here we sat. I didn't care that the movie was on mute. I didn't care about anything at the moment. Onscreen, Vincent Price continued terrorizing his guests in what I recognized as *The House on Haunted Hill*. My eyes were pointed in the general direction of the TV, but I wasn't watching.

Thoughts were tumbling through my head, but I was so tired that nothing seemed to make sense. Should I be feeling fear over the disappearance of *Y Ddraig Goch?* Sadness over Fehr's long and lonely life? Peace that he'd finally left this world? Who knew. I turned to Gil, hoping his veteran's wisdom could clear up the confusion I was feeling.

Instead, I found myself asking, "Why are you afraid of ghosts?"

The question had been bothering me since the moment we'd crossed Callowleigh's threshold. Gil, a man I would generally describe as walking the Earth without fear, had been reduced to frozen terror on more than one occasion that evening. It didn't make sense and the question had been gnawing at me all night. Sea monsters, demons, satanic rituals, and snakes. None of it bothered him.

But ghosts did.

He looked up at the screen vacantly. After a moment he sighed. "You know that you were hired as a replacement for a man named Parker, right?"

I nodded.

He took a slow bite of pizza, his jaw working over the doughy crust in silence. "And you know that he was killed on the job, right?"

Again, I nodded.

Gil dropped his remaining crust into the shell of the box and grabbed a fresh piece. He spoke, but he still stared straight ahead at the muted television.

"Before Parker was a man named Grayson. He was killed on the job, as well. Even Grayson wasn't the first. Did you know that?"

I shook my head.

He nodded soberly. "I've been doing this for a long time. A long, long time. Fighting monsters, trying to make a difference. I've seen a lot of people die, both good and bad. I've buried too many friends and family. Far too many, really." He looked at me, his eyes glassy. "Any man who has done what I've done and lived the life I've lived would be crazy not to fear ghosts. Ghosts are spirits of the dead that remain after death because of 'unfinished business,' right?" He shrugged. "Everybody knows that. But it's never good stuff. It's always because of horrible, sad stories. Like Fehr's story. That's... that's normal, I'm sorry to say. And everyday I dread seeing the ghost of someone I love. It would break my heart if... if someone I loved was cursed with such a fate."

Someone like your wife, I thought. The idea made even my heart ache.

"I hope you never fear ghosts," he said. "It is a terrible thing. Really." He took a bite of pizza, his jaw moving slowly.

I opened my mouth to speak, hoping to offer some condolence, some comfort. Hell, even some genuine thanks for his honesty and care.

I opened my mouth to speak, and as I did, the door behind me opened. I heard footsteps and turned.

A thin, pale, and freckled young man was stumbling through the doorway, lipstick on his cheek and neck. It was Finch, the third and final Zero.

"Where the hell have you been, young man?" Gil said, turning. "I've been worried sick!"

"Shhhh," Finch said, raising a finger to his lips.

Gil smiled. "Wine?"

Finch shook his head. "Gin." He smiled, a display of emotion uncharacteristic of our stoic partner. "And I met a woman," he said gesturing at his disheveled appearance. "As you can see."

Gil smiled again. "Any date that gets you home at six AM can't have been that bad."

"Truth." Finch nodded. "You can tell me about your slow evening at the library later, I need sleep." He bowed dramatically. "Gentlemen, I bid you a good evening." He walked down the hallway and closed his door softly behind him.

Gil turned to me. "It's good to be home again, isn't it?"

"Yes, it is." I missed my own bed, but there was something about being with Finch and Gil. I'd only known the men for a short while, but it felt right. It felt like... family.

"I have to go to sleep," I said. "I'm exhausted." I stood and began walking towards one of the multitude of guest rooms.

"Oh, one last thing," Gil said. "While I was waiting for my pizza, I pulled a couple of favors and figured out who hired Jane Julius to steal the *Ddraig Goch*. Turns out I still got a *little* pull left in this town."

I groaned, and cracked my neck. "Oh yeah? Who was it?"

"Some guy named Roach," Gil said, shrugging. "I never heard of 'im. How bout you?"

He glanced over his shoulder at me. "No," I said. "Doesn't ring a bell."

It was the first time I'd lied to Gil.

I walked to bed, feeling that old dread forming in the pit of my stomach once again. *Nothing's easy,* I thought. I had so hoped *Y Ddraig Goch* was gone. Wrong again. It was only a matter of time before the damn thing resurfaced. Well, shit. And I had really been looking forward to a good night's sleep.

Unfortunately, you can't always get what you want.

THE END!

Thus concludes the short introduction to the world of the Zeros. Further tales are soon to come!

Please visit http://www.gilsgrimoire.com for more information about upcoming adventures with Gil, Finch, and Dylan.

Thank you for reading.
–E.B

GIL'S GRIMOIRE: VOLUME ONE PREVIEW

Thanks for reading the novella
Two Zeros and The Library of Doom!
the introduction to Gil's Grimoire.

Now enjoy Chapter One to the inaugural Volume of
Gil's Grimoire, the first full-length novel of the
Zeros:

The Zeros and The Man Who Could Not Die
by Eric Bonkowski

Available now!

CHAPTER 1. THE ZEROS

The revenant battle was over–my very first, although undoubtedly not my last–and Finch was speaking in a mind-numbing ninety-five year old college professor monotone, complete with the hint of an English accent. Ironic in this case, considering he looked like one of those twenty-something hipster kids from Brooklyn.

"Oftentimes, it is the lack of any truly conclusive evidence that will perpetuate natural earthborn doubt. The doubt–along with a fair dose of stubborn fear–is enough to keep even the most inquisitive minds at ease. However, when confronted with hard physical evidence, even the most skeptical mind cannot ignore fact, regardless of how inexplicable. I call this the 'evidentiary silver bullet.' I think this evening was your silver bullet, Dylan."

Gil spoke up, giggling. "Got that right! Our boy's got hard physical evidence splattered all over him!"

Gil Abercrombie. Eccentric billionaire, monster hunter, and exuberant manchild. Aficionado of pipes, scale science fiction models, and Hawaiian shirts. Alistair Finch. Coldly logical, monster hunter, and know-it-all boy-genius assistant. Enjoys frowning, fine Scotch whiskey, and indecipherable foreign films. They were friends to the lonesome and desperate; villains to the undead and malicious.

To backtrack a little, either one of these guys could have dropped a few hints in the original job offer I received so that I would perhaps have been a bit more prepared for how my life was about to turn into an insane circus funhouse. They hadn't.

The note had read: <u>The Docks. Midnight. Come armed.</u>

Cryptic, minimalist, and dramatic. To call it a job description was generous, but the certified check folded inside the note helped me swallow my questions along with the lingering doubt. If it hadn't been a certified check, I would have immediately torn it up and thrown it out along with my mounting credit card bills and junk mail. If it hadn't been certified, it would have had to be a joke. The damn check had more numbers than the note did words. I decided to give the note the benefit of the doubt. You have to admit; a few extra decimal points can be persuasive.

I'd been laid off four days earlier from the private security firm where I'd been working for the past six years. Not bad money, but I had to wear a suit with a logo on the breast and spend ten hours a day checking IDs and putting up wet floor signs when it rained. Getting canned was probably a blessing in disguise. I'd spent my handful of unemployed days watching daytime television and reading murder mysteries. Daytime television is a nice reminder that being at work isn't so bad.

I arrived at the dock early, taking a cab from the Broad Street line's last subway stop. In Philadelphia, the harbor overlooked the Delaware River, a churning snake of black water that had once been a busy import/export route. Now, it was mostly deserted. These days, the only things you'd likely find in the Delaware would be bags of trash and maybe a few stray jumpers from the Walt Whitman Bridge. In the pale moonlight, huge bodies of empty ships rose and fell along the water's edge as the tide lapped at their rusted hulls. Behind me, a long line of warehouses stood against the dock and the shoreline, most of them abandoned. In the distance I could hear the low foghorn of a passing tanker. I felt like an extra in a shitty film noire.

A deep rumbling of music announced my new employer's arrival. A brown hulking mammoth of a car circa 1955 was burping clouds of exhaust up into the starry night sky. Inside, what sounded like some epic power metal was rattling the car's windows. I guess you could call it music. Through the glass, I could hear a wailing guitar solo and some high, screechy vocals. The driver bobbed his head in time. After a moment, the engine sputtered to a grinding halt.

A tall, lanky man emerged from the driver's

side wearing raggedy jeans and a yellow, purple, orange, and green Tiki shirt complete with girls in grass skirts and palm trees. It was hideous, like some Deadhead had thrown up on him. On his feet, he wore huge white orthopedic sneakers better suited for someone double his age. He had salt and pepper hair down to his shoulders and a thick bushy mustache that half-covered his mouth.

"Hey, hey, you must be Dylan," he said to me, grinning. "You look like you could rip a phonebook in half, my man. Perfecto."

I'm big. I mean, damn big. I never really worked out, but I'm still pretty built. People assume I'm a linebacker or bouncer when they meet me. In this case, I think it got me the job. They also usually assume I have the IQ of a microwave oven.

"You must be Mr. Abercrombie," I said, extending my hand.

He shook it enthusiastically. I'd eventually learn that my boss did everything enthusiastically. "Call me Gil. If somebody calls me Mr. Abercrombie then I figure they either want me to make a donation to their university or become a Scientologist."

"Okay, Gil," I said. "Is this your... associate?"

He turned and laid his hand across the battered car's roof. "No, this is my baby," he said. "The Tank. A real classic. 1960 Mercedes 190B. Vintage collector's car, here. This puppy is worth a fair chunk of change, lemme tell you." I tried to look impressed as I admired the rust stains blooming from the wheel wells, the three missing hubcaps, and the dents that covered the car like polka dots.

"Actually, I meant your other associate." I pointed to the slim kid stepping from the passenger's side. He was a tad under six foot and skinny, dressed head to toe in black, making his red hair all the more glaring. His face was pale and freckled just under his eyes, which were dark and deep. Perhaps he was the artist of the group.

"Oh, this isn't my associate, this is my *partner*," Gil said. "Finch, come say hello."

"Hello," Finch said with a nod as he rounded The Tank and opened the trunk.

"He's very serious," Gil said. "I mean we *are* on a mission. Savin' the innocent, defeatin' evil monsters, etc, etc." He shrugged, grinning. "After this we'll probably hit up some Mexican food or somethin'."

"Hold on. A mission? Your job description left a little to be desired."

"That's why I included the check, big man."

"Well, yeah, that's–"

"Wait, wait, wait! Hold on!" Gil interrupted, waving his hands. "I didn't do the job interview yet. We don't take just any slouch. Are you ready?"

"Um..."

"Number one: Can you drive?"

"Yeah, sure I–"

"Nice! And number two. This one's a real doozy, okay?" He licked his lips. "Can you cook?"

"Actually, I love to–"

"Fantastic! Here's what I like. Spaghetti-os, tacos, sloppy joes, grilled cheese, hot pockets, nachos, fried chicken, mac and cheese, hot dogs, that pink wine that comes in boxes..."

"Am I your... butler?" I interrupted.

"What? No. I mean, not really. You're an equal partner, just like Finch here, of course. I'm here for morale, Finch for the laughs, and you can be the cook. Come on, the fact that you cook is pretty great."

"Well, what exactly are you paying me to do? What is it you do, exactly?"

Gil smiled. "This is that really awkward moment of the first job where you ask a bunch of totally fair questions because you're beginning to wonder what you got yourself into and I try to answer them without scaring you away. You know, the whole what's goin' on here, what do you do here, blah, blah, blah thing. Let's just skip it, eh?"

Oh boy.

"I see that look on your face, and it's totally fair. I mean, you deserve to know what's up. I get that, big man. But I picked you because I hear you're smart and you're discreet." Gil rounded The Tank and stood at Finch's side in front of the open trunk. "So trust me when I say this isn't the first time I've trained somebody this way, and believe me, this way is much easier. Just roll with it, okay?"

"Roll with it?"

"Yeah," he smiled. "Roll with it." He pulled a

huge, weathered tome from the trunk along with a flashlight and dropped them into a duffel bag Finch was holding open. Across the book's leather jacket, the words *GIL'S GRIMOIRE* were stamped crookedly.

"If you start to get spooked or lose your nerve, just keep that check in mind. You'll be getting one of those every month."

"Every *month*?"

"You got that right, big man. It's worth it for us heroes!" He struck an honest-to-God Superman pose.

"Zeros is more like it," Finch said. His voice was bitter in the cool night air. "Worth nothing to no one, we are." He winked at me.

Gil smacked Finch's arm like a disap-proving grandmother. "Stop being dramatic, Mr. Grump. This is supposed to be fun, remember?" I saw the glint of moonlight on metal as he pulled something from the trunk.

"Uh, is that a sword...?"

Gil either couldn't hear me or ignored me. He chattered on as he pulled another long, impeccable blade free and dropped it nonchalantly into Finch's bag. "It's gonna be pretty awesome, dukin' it out with some revenants. Remember, if we get done early enough, the burritos are on me." He looked up at me; I must've had shock in my eyes. "Just some swords, dude, relax. Haven't you ever rocked out a renaissance fair? Anyway, this is gonna be a cakewalk."

The last thing he pulled from the trunk was a weathered skull covered in crooked runes. Gil rubbed his hand across the surface like a Magic 8 Ball. "Do us proud tonight, old buddy," he said before dropping the skull into Finch's duffel. Finch shouldered the bag and leaned into the trunk, pulling out a longsword and leaving the leather sheath behind. Gil reached in and pulled a double-sided battle ax free with a cackle.

He looked up at me. "Oh, damn, I'm sorry. Where are my manners?" From the duffle on Finch's shoulder, he dug out a blade, shorter than the others, and the only weapon with noticeable nicks cut into the edge. He held it out to me, hilt first. "Short sword?"

ABOUT THE AUTHOR

Eric Bonkowski lives in Delaware. He is inspired daily by Saturday afternoon cliffhanger serials, classic comics and comic strips, and horror films of the '30s and '40s–to say nothing of mystery, fantasy, and science fiction pulp writings of every age.

He spends his time reading, watching campy movies, and writing, supported all the while by his remarkable wife and family. During the rare quieter moments, he can be found listening to jazz and falling asleep well before bedtime.

He is the author of the *Gil's Grimoire* series and the *Brick Brannigan* series.

Visit him at:

http://www.gilsgrimoire.com

http://www.brickbrannigan.com